The Dead Don't Lie

A Harbour Bay Novel

Camille Taylor

The Dead Don't Lie

Limitless Publishing, LLC
Kailua, HI 96734
www.limitlesspublishing.com

Formatting: Limitless Publishing

ISBN-13: 978-1-68058-541-4
ISBN-10: 1-68058-541-X

Prologue

Someone was behind her.

Footsteps echoed loudly as she ran. Louisa Burnes stumbled, the heel of her stiletto snapping. She caught herself before she fell, scraping the delicate skin of her palm against the graffiti-covered brick wall beside her. She cursed as the first signs of the sting registered.

She ran faster than before, terrified of what might happen should she be caught. She was all alone in the early morning hours, everyone else asleep in their warm beds. No one would hear her screams.

Her breath came out in quick bursts, her natural blonde hair whipping about her face as she moved. She shivered, despite the warm breeze and sweat trickled down her back. Her heart in her throat, she staggered in the direction of her car, parked further down the street.

The pounding of feet on the pavement had fear liquefying her insides. The shot of adrenaline did nothing to the drug taking effect, already slowing her down, making her groggy. She was usually so careful, and now she was terrified the lack of caution would be her last mistake.

Please God, she begged. *Let me get out of this.*

She would go to church with her mother, mend her relationship with her sister, if only she could get away unscathed.

If only she knew who the pursuer was. They'd been following her since she left the club, had made no attempt to call out to her, and when she had started running, they kept up with her.

She tightened her grip on her keys, the metal edges biting into her palm.

Just a little longer, she told herself as she took shortcut after shortcut. She'd parked farther away so no one would link her to the club, afraid for her reputation. She wished she hadn't cared.

Louisa's eyes blurred. Tears streaked down her cheeks. She kept moving, down alleyways and past stinking dumpsters. If only it wasn't too late to turn around and head back to the club, but she'd already gone too far to turn back. She would lose precious minutes. It was best to keep going, if she could.

She placed her hand on the brick wall of the building beside her, in an attempt to stop the dizziness flooding her head. Keeping her fingertips on the cool motionless brick, she moved further down the alley, looking for the exit.

I have to hurry.

The world spun and she wondered why this was happening and why she'd been drugged.

She never accepted drinks from strangers, so she wasn't sure when she'd ingested the drug.

She had worked until six, an early night, before going to her mother's house for dinner. Later, she had gone to the club as she always did. But she hadn't drunk anything she hadn't before and was certain there hadn't been an opportunity to spike her drink, nor had she been injected with anything—at least not that she could remember, her brain already losing huge chunks of the night. Her worry increased ten-fold and fear was almost a physical presence beside her.

Rounding a corner, she realised nothing looked familiar. Panic surged through her.

The assailant was almost upon her. She forced herself to move, wondering which way to go. She wanted to scream in frustration. She chose left and continued on until she finally came to a dead end. She was trapped. It was all over.

I should've gone the other way.

A sharp pain burned, the blade slicing through her flesh. She screamed and turned her back against the wall, facing her attacker. Her eyes widened when her chin lifted and she found the familiar face.

Oh my God.

The hand came down again, the knife once more piercing her soft skin. She fell to the dirty, foul smelling ground. The world went dark and warm blood pooled beneath her body. Her blood. She only had one more thought before she died, taking the identity of her killer to the grave.

Aimee.

Chapter 1

The phone chirped beside the bed. Detective Sergeant James Hawke groaned and rolled over in bed, groping for his mobile phone as he glanced at the digital clock's display that glowed red in the darkness. He'd been up late the night before unpacking and wasn't due in to work for another four hours so the interruption was unexpected.

For years, he'd wanted to work in the city, coming from a small town, and he supposed now that he'd accepted the detective position at Harbour Bay's LAC—Local Area Command—he would have to get used to the disrupted sleep. While Harbour Bay wasn't a metropolis like Melbourne or Sydney, it was large enough to suit his needs for the time being. He cleared his throat before answering.

He was told to meet his new partner, Darryl Hill in an alley out in the industrial area off Border Street. He dropped the phone onto the crumpled sheets and slipped from the bed.

He showered quickly before dressing in one of the suits hanging in his wardrobe. They weren't

Hugo Boss but they were practical. Dark fabric slacks, a light grey shirt and a black tie was all he needed, foregoing his jacket. It may be springtime in Harbour Bay but it was hot as hell and if the heat didn't get you, the humidity would. He brushed his brown hair, which had been lightened by the sun over the years, and then cleaned his teeth before grabbing his gun holster, badge, and keys.

In just under thirty minutes he was pulling up outside the alley. The scene was cast in early morning grey, pink, and yellow as the rising sun peeked through the gaps between the warehouses.

James parked his car and made his way towards the blue and white chequered police tape. His gaze swept over the scene. A red unmarked police Commodore blocked the westbound entrance. Beside it sat three police issued vehicles, each with red and blue lights flashing. A uniformed officer stood at the entrance to the alley.

He stepped aside to allow the coroner's van to pass, pausing beside the officer guarding the crime scene. An older gentleman in his late fifties or early sixties retrieved the gurney from the back of his vehicle before rolling it into the alley, slipping beneath the tape that the officer held up for him.

He flashed his badge and identification to the uniformed officer and stated his name. The officer nodded, and made a note on the clipboard he held. When he was done, he pointed towards the end of the alley. James could see the body of a young woman on the ground.

He strode purposely towards the victim, taking in the scene as he went. The forensics' team was busy collecting evidence as James glanced over at a smartly dressed woman leaning against the brick wall of the alley. Her dark hair was pulled severely back at the base of her neck. His gaze fell to her waist and the holster and badged clipped there. She didn't look up as she continued to speak quietly into her mobile.

He stopped when he reached the body. The coroner was busy surveying the remains. He spoke to the man crouched beside the victim who dutifully took notes.

"Detective Hill?" he asked.

The man's head turned and shrewd brown eyes assessed him.

"Yes, that's right. Darryl Hill. You must be James Hawke." Detective Hill stood in one lithe motion and extended his hand.

He was a tall man, almost six-foot. James took the man's hand and shook firmly.

His gaze swept over his new partner with the skill and ease of a seasoned cop. Hill, like him, was dressed in a suit minus the jacket. His tie had been clipped with a small Australian Flag pin, and his light brown hair was neatly combed to one side. He would have guessed Darryl was in his early to mid-thirties.

"What do we have?" James asked, eager to begin. He'd requested the transfer because he didn't want to spend his entire life writing speeding tickets, breaking up bar fights, and attending vehicular accidents. He wanted to solve crimes. There just wasn't much need for it back in his hometown of about twenty-thousand.

Darryl recited the facts. "Female. Thirty years of age. Stabbed five times. I.D. says she's Louisa Burnes."

"Is she local?"

Darryl nodded. "Donovan's locating the address of the next of kin as we speak. It seems she was chased here by her attacker. She's been dead at least three hours. But I'm waiting on Doctor Stone here to confirm."

James greeted the doctor before turning to the victim. Dressed in expensive clothes marred by blood, the heel of one shoe broken, she looked out of place. His gaze swept the alley. "What was she doing in this neighbourhood?"

Darryl tucked his notepad into his pocket. "That's what we're here to find out."

The woman he'd seen earlier appeared by his side. "Hey, Hill, got that next of kin. Mother, Ruth Burnes. Here's her address." She ripped a piece of paper from her notepad and handed it to him. "She's all yours."

Darryl glared at her. "I believe it's your turn to talk to the next of kin."

"I'm just giving you the practice," she told him with a scowl.

"Donovan, meet the new guy," Darryl said.

She extended a hand towards him. "Amelia Donovan, Detective Inspector. I'll be working on this case with you and Hill."

"James Hawke, a pleasure."

A glint appeared in her dark eyes and she grinned at him.

"That will soon change," Darryl said.

Amelia made a dismissing motion with her hands. "Ignore him. I'm not all that bad."

Darryl scoffed. "You have no secrets, *Mia*. Kellie has told me everything."

Amelia rolled her eyes. "Highly doubtful, Hill. Kellie knows when to keep her mouth shut and she would never betray an understanding."

Darryl's gaze fell on James. "Kellie is my wife," he explained.

"And my best friend," she added.

The two detectives verbally sparred with one another. There was affection beneath the barbs. They'd obviously known each other for some time and it clearly showed. James hoped that he too would find a home here.

"That must get awkward," he said.

Amelia shrugged. "Only sometimes."

Darryl glanced at the body of Louisa Burnes before turning to Amelia. "You'll finish up here?" When she nodded, he turned to James. "All right then, let's go talk to Mrs. Burnes."

Chapter 2

The house, painted an off-white colour, was situated in a quiet cul-de-sac in a blue collar neighbourhood, and the lawn was impeccably maintained. This was a woman who took pride in her home and garden. Ruth Burnes had gone into the kitchen to prepare tea after leading them into the family room. James's gaze explored the small cosy room. The furniture was old but in good condition. It reminded him of his grandmother's house— except for the crucifix adorning the wall beside the painting of the Virgin Mary.

A side table held a collection of framed photographs and he studied them closely. Several were of two little girls, both pretty blondes with wide smiles. They looked like little dolls. He moved to another photograph and recognised a young and attractive Ruth Burnes with the two girls. He frowned when he found no picture of the husband and father among the collection.

Ruth returned with a serving tray laden with three china cups and a teapot.

She was around sixty years old, her hair grey, and she made no attempt to hide her age with make-up. Her flower-patterned dress hung at knee-length. He made a move to relieve her of the tray but she kindly refused. She sat down on the sofa across from them and leaned forward to pour them each a cup of tea.

James thanked her.

"Thank you, Mrs. Burnes," Darryl said. "Again, I'm very sorry for your loss."

Ruth sat regally on the sofa and took a sip of tea before answering. "Thank you, Detectives. I pray her soul finds salvation."

Darryl flipped open a notepad. "Mrs. Burnes, do you know of anyone who might want to hurt your daughter?"

"No. Louisa was a wonderful child. So loving and sweet, always head of the class. She never did anything to anybody. I don't understand how this could happen."

"She was a lawyer. Did she take on any cases that may have upset anyone?"

Ruth shook her head. "No. Louisa was an estate lawyer. Wills and probate, that kind of thing. She dealt mostly with paperwork and grieving families. She was wonderful like that."

"Do you know if Louisa had any boyfriends?" James asked.

Ruth took another sip of her tea. "No. She never talked about men. Not to me, anyway. She knew my opinion on affairs outside of marriage. If she told anyone, she might have told Aimee, but it's unlikely."

"Aimee?" Darryl asked.

"My younger daughter." Ruth rose and lifted the photo from a side table, handing it to Darryl.

It was the photo James had been looking at, showing two little girls of about eight and ten. They wore white dresses with matching knee high socks. It occurred to James that none of the photos in the room showed the girls when they were older.

"Do you know where we can find your daughter?" Darryl asked.

Ruth's face hardened and she played with the cross hanging around her neck. "She owns an establishment here in town."

Chapter 3

James followed Darryl inside. Above, the neon pink sign flashed *Club X*. They moved towards a podium just inside the door that reminded James of a hostess's stand in a fancy restaurant. A woman stood behind it, her make-up drawing attention to the unusual shape of her eyes and her full red lips. She wore a dark blue business skirt that reached her knees and a red blouse that was unbuttoned enough to reveal a matching lace bra.

The walls of the club, housed in an old warehouse, had been painted dark red complementing the mahogany wood floorboards, the universal décor of brothels the world over, and James knew from the exterior that the club spanned several hundred square meters. However, unlike other sex clubs, this one projected class and catered to high-end clients. He glanced to his right through an archway and saw a large room with low line sofas and a stocked bar off to the side. One woman wore a stewardess's outfit while she sat beside a man in a suit on the couch, her hand stroking his thigh as he talked and she listened, her stare never leaving his face.

A man dressed in a construction worker costume, his oiled chest bare, slipped behind the bar and filled a glass for a female patron before taking her hand and then tucking some of her dark hair behind her ear. She giggled and leaned in to his touch.

James focused on the attractive woman behind the podium. She lifted her head from the ledger in front of her as they approached, offering a welcoming smile.

"Hello, and welcome to Club X. How may I help you?" Her voice was throaty and seductive, and James wondered if this was a performance to entice male customers. It had the desired effect as his own body reacted to it and he fought to rein it in.

Darryl produced his badge. "Detective Hill and Hawke, we're from the LAC. We're looking for Aimee Burnes."

Her demeanour changed, losing any trace of friendliness. "Unbelievable," she said, frowning. "I just got through an inspection. You may not believe it, but I run a legal establishment and have up-to-date paperwork and licences." She planted her hands on her hips. "I'm sick of being harassed and if you don't start leaving me alone, I'm going to file a complaint. All I'm doing here is providing clean and harmless entertainment."

She glared at them, her breasts rising with each deep, agitated breath she took. He caught the movement and it took every ounce of his willpower to raise his gaze to her face. James noted her voice continued to hold the same seductive qualities as before, even in anger and wished he hadn't. It did nothing to alleviate his current condition and he hoped like hell nobody noticed.

"You're Aimee Burnes?"

James noticed his partner give her a once over as if trying to reconcile the sweet looking kid in the photo with the alluring siren before them.

Aimee gritted her teeth. "Yes."

James studied the woman who looked nothing like the girl she had been. The only feature that said they were talking to the right woman was her grey almond-shaped eyes, so much like the eyes of the dead woman. They must've come from the absentee father, since Ruth Burnes had baby blues.

The blonde hair had been replaced with a dark chestnut that stopped just a few inches short of her waist, the long tresses straight and cut into artful layers. Tendrils of her hair had fallen over her shoulder and down the swell of her high, firm breast. Gone was the prepubescent body and in its place were curves and dips that he was sure sent every man into lust. Him included. He rubbed his sweat slickened palm over the fabric of his pants.

"We're not here about your club," Darryl said.

Aimee's eyebrow rose in curiosity.

"We're here about your sister, Louisa Burnes," James told her.

Aimee's gaze flicked between them. The impact as he met her eyes hit him hard in the gut.

"Is there somewhere we can talk in private, Ms. Burnes?"

Aimee turned towards a blonde standing just inside the archway nearby. "Tiffany!"

The younger woman walked over, clad in a nurse's outfit, her curly blonde hair bouncing as she moved. "Yeah?"

"Tiff, can you look after the front for me?"

"Sure. Take your time."

"We can talk in my office," Aimee told them.

They followed her into a plain office in the back, and James blinked, surprised. The beige walls were completely out of place along with the rich royal blue carpet. It looked like the office of a high powered executive, not some madam of what he could only assume was a pricey whorehouse. Aimee sat behind her mahogany desk as he and Darryl each took one of the chairs designated for visitors.

"So what has Louisa done?" she asked, once they were seated.

"Louisa is dead."

Aimee's lips parted on an exhale of breath. Beneath the heavy make-up she wore, her face paled.

"What? When?" she asked, shock evident in her voice.

"Last night."

Tears sprang into her eyes and she blinked furiously. She turned away for a moment and swallowed hard. "I see. Does my mother know?"

"We spoke to her earlier," James said.

Her face hardened. "Yes, of course you have. Not that she would bother telling me. May I ask how? Was it some sort of accident?"

James studied her reaction closely as Darryl spoke. "She was murdered."

"Murdered?" Her hand rose to rest above her

heart. "There has to be a mistake. How? Why?"

"She was stabbed. Her body was found earlier this morning not far from here. As for why, we're still investigating."

James allowed Darryl to take point. Not only was his partner the lead on the case, but he was also the more experienced detective and James had no problem taking a back seat. They were both after the same thing. To find the killer. That was all that mattered. And that took teamwork. He also found it hard to concentrate. Aimee's pain was palpable despite trying hard to keep her emotions under control in their presence.

She took a steadying breath, the exhale shaky which belied her calm. "No. That can't be." She shook her head vehemently. "You're sure the victim is my sister? Maybe I should I.D. her, just to be positive."

"She has already been identified," Darryl said softly. "I'm sorry, but there has been no mistake. The victim is most definitely Louisa Burnes of Applewood Street."

"Oh God. Jesus Christ, how could this have happened?"

James raised his eyebrows at her blatant blasphemy. After seeing the house she had grown up in, he had expected some sort of decorum, but then again, she did own a sex club. He shared a glance with his partner and read the same surprise on his face.

"Ms. Burnes, would you mind answering a few questions about your sister?" he asked. James's chest tightened and an ache began beneath the surface. He forced himself not to rub directly over his heart in an effort to relieve the pressure.

"What kind of questions?"

Darryl spoke next. "Do you know of anyone who might want to harm your sister?"

Aimee leaned back in her chair. "Not to my knowledge, though I'm not entirely sure Louisa would tell me if there was. We were never really close. Our mother made sure of that. She was the good sister and I was the bad one."

"She never mentioned any troubles at work or with a friend?"

"No. We tend to keep our own counsel." She stood and walked across the room, her hips swaying slightly as she moved. She stopped, staring at the wall. Her shoulders rose and fell heavily with every breath. "I'm beginning to regret that and the answer to your next question is no, I didn't notice a change in behaviour or anything out of the ordinary."

Darryl took out a pen and notepad from his pocket. "Did your sister ever come here? For recreation, that is."

"If your sister owned a club like mine, wouldn't you?" she asked.

Darryl cleared his throat. "Is that a yes?""

She turned to face them, her arms crossed beneath her breasts.

"Yes, although you won't find anything on her credit card. Louisa always paid cash. She had an image to uphold and a mother to keep happy. As to what she did inside my club…" Aimee shrugged. "I can't tell you."

Darryl nodded. "Do you know if Louisa had any

boyfriends?"

Aimee fingered the bracelet around her slender wrist. "No, Louisa didn't have boyfriends. She was very involved with her career and didn't have time for anyone or anything."

"Can anyone verify your whereabouts last night and earlier this morning?"

Her startled gaze jumped between him and Darryl as the meaning of the question sank in.

"I was working and didn't leave until closing, after I cleared the premises and locked up. I assume many can vouch for me, however nights are our busiest time, often chaotic. I couldn't begin to give you names."

Darryl wrote in the notepad as James studied Aimee's expressions. If she was lying, she was a master at it. He hadn't detected any deception in her replies.

She swallowed. "Am I a suspect?"

"Should you be?"

Her fingers curled into a fist, as if she'd just become aware of her actions and had to force herself to stop.

"No. I would never hurt Louisa."

"Good. We're just covering our bases. When was the last time you saw your sister?"

"Here. A couple of nights ago, I think," she said. "I'm not sure."

"You don't remember?" James pressed.

"No. To the outside world, my club is pleasure and fantasy but to me it's a job, with payroll and expenditures and tax forms. When I'm not greeting clients, I spend most of my time in my office."

"Did any of your employees have any issues with her? Any problems you're aware of?"

"Not to my knowledge. But if there was a problem I'm sure they would've brought it to my attention. They're very loyal to me."

James raised an eyebrow. "Really?"

Aimee shrugged. "Why not? The pay is good. They get overtime, sick pay, and annual leave. They're in a union and they don't get beat up. Better than being on the streets. They're safe in my club and they know it. I don't tolerate violence of any sort. They're free to accept or decline any offers."

Darryl stood. "Thank you for your time."

Aimee shook both their hands and walked them to the door. "I would appreciate it if you'd keep me updated. Anything I can do to help, please let me know."

"We will, Ms. Burnes, and please accept our sympathy. Should you need it, I can supply the name of a good grief counsellor," Darryl offered.

"I'll let you know. And you know where to find me if you have any more questions."

Darryl produced a business card from his pocket. "Should you remember something before we meet again, give us a call."

"I will, Detective."

Chapter 4

Aimee closed the door behind them and leaned heavily against it before sliding to the floor. She stared at the wall of her office as she tried to make sense of things.

Louisa was dead. Murdered.

It was no mistake. She'd been positively identified, and this wasn't some cruel joke.

How could this be happening? It was so unreal she couldn't get her brain to fully grasp it. The last time she'd seen Louisa, her sister had been happy and healthy, and now she was gone. A whisper raced across her mind.

Dead.

Murdered.

Aimee shook uncontrollably as grief overwhelmed her. She pushed back the sob rising in her throat and blinked away the tears stinging her eyes. Crying never fixed anything. Nothing could fix this situation.

Louisa was gone.

She drew in a ragged breath as she tried to rein in

her emotions, burying her head in her hands. She replayed the last conversation she had with her sister. Louisa had been pushing to forget the past. To make peace. As if that would ever happen. Especially now that Louisa was gone. She was the only one who'd cared that the Burnes family was fractured.

Ruth certainly didn't. After all, she was the one who'd made it so.

She shuddered when she thought of her mother, who hadn't been in the best of health to begin with. This could kill her. When Louisa had told her about their mother's declining health, Aimee had been surprised. She thought the old bitch too mean to be struck down. She'd been wrong. Not that her mother would be dying soon, but each day she was weakening and might not last more than five years.

Would she mourn her mother as she did her sister? Probably not, because she'd grieved for her mother years ago, grieved for the love that had never been there and how easily her mother had tossed her aside.

Aimee contemplated calling her, reaching out, but immediately dismissed the idea. She was in no position to offer sympathy or a shoulder to cry on and her mother wouldn't accept any of those from her even if she was.

Her mother had never warmed to her. It wasn't a figment of her imagination. Ruth had told her numerous times that she wished Aimee had never been born. She made no bones on showing her younger daughter how she truly felt. Once it had hurt her, but now she was used to meaning nothing to the woman who had given her life.

Aimee hugged her arms around her raised legs and rested her head on her knees. Pain washed over her and pierced her heart until she was struggling to breathe. She'd never been close with her sister but that didn't mean she wanted any harm to come to her. She swallowed hard at what it must've been like for her sister, scared and alone, knowing no one would come to her rescue—that she would die. Aimee squeezed her arms tighter around her legs in an effort to provide herself comfort.

It was what she'd been doing for most of her life. Comforting herself because she knew she couldn't count on anyone else.

She was alone.

Truly alone. She hadn't appreciated her sister while she had the chance and now she would never be able to change that.

It was an opportunity lost.

She fought against the sorrow weighing heavily on her. Aimee pushed away from the floor. It would do no good to wallow in misery. She could change nothing and feeling sad would only pull her down into the dark abyss of depression.

Her breath left her in a loud exhale as she caught her reflection in the mirror she'd affixed to the wall in an attempt to make her office look larger. Her eyes were stormy with emotion she refused to shed, her skin pale even beneath the foundation she wore. Beyond that, she saw her sister. She touched her jaw. She and Louisa had looked identical for years, with their sandy blonde hair and grey eyes. Aimee had eradicated all of the similarities years ago when she'd left Harbour Bay for Sydney.

She'd gone from one side of the colour spectrum to the next and dyed her hair raven black. Then she'd begun to cover her face with make-up. Anything to change until she couldn't even recognise herself. Her mother had never condoned make-up or nail polish. She admitted she'd gone a little overboard but for the first time in her life she'd been able to do as she wished and without judgement. Or at least, none she cared about.

It had been the most freeing experience of her life. The most beneficial. Over the years, she'd become more comfortable with herself, with her past, and she'd transformed back to her old self. But she'd never returned to her blonde roots, much preferring the darker shade that drew attention to her eyes and made them sparkle.

She blinked moisture away, unable to keep from dwelling on all she had lost. Why had she been so stubborn? Her sister had gone to her grave believing Aimee wanted nothing to do with her. That couldn't be more wrong. Louisa was her older sister. She'd been there her entire life. Maybe not always on her side, but she'd looked up to her sister. Idolised her. Aimee couldn't believe she'd never see her again. She shivered and rubbed her hands up and down her arms to ward off the chill.

What the hell had happened? Why had Louisa been taken from her?

She hadn't been lying to the detectives when she'd said her sister was the sweetest, kindest woman she knew. Louisa had led an uninteresting life. She made no ripples. If anyone should've been a target, it was Aimee, since she dealt with less than favourable people on a daily basis.

Life rarely made sense.

She didn't know what to do. Should she be calling someone to arrange the funeral? How long would it take for Louisa's body to be released? She hadn't thought to ask the detectives. Should she enquire? The older one had given her his card. What was the protocol for homicide investigations?

She sank heavily into the chair behind her desk. She felt a million years old. Her energy—her very essence—sapped from her body.

She glanced at her phone and then decided against making the call. Her mother wouldn't appreciate her interference. Even if it alleviated Ruth's stress levels and allowed her time to grieve.

She blew out another shaky breath and leaned back in her chair, closing her eyes against the agony she felt. Thousands of questions floated inside her head. The most persistent was, could she have prevented this tragedy?

Chapter 5

"Do you believe Ms. Burnes's death has something to do with the club?" James asked as they stepped into the elevator at the LAC, the four-storey, light brown building overlooking the harbour and further out to the Tasman Sea. Formidable, a once convict barrack, the L-shaped fortress was as unaesthetically pleasing as possible, as if it had been a particular mission of the architect.

Darryl punched the button for the second level. "It's certainly a possibility. Especially when you consider she was found a few blocks away. You tell me, Hawke."

"More than likely. What's your take on the sister?"

Darryl leaned against the wall of the carriage. "On the surface, she appeared to have all the expected emotions—shock, disbelief, grief, anger. I'm inclined to believe her for now, until I have evidence to suggest otherwise."

He agreed. Aimee Burnes hardly seemed the type to run a bordello. He thought she'd look older and worn beyond her years with a jaded expression in her eyes. He hadn't anticipated the young, beautiful, charismatic woman he'd found. He could understand her success. She was alluring. Even in business attire, she exuded sex. He knew it wasn't forced and if he had to guess, it came naturally to her.

He remembered the way Mrs. Burnes had told them about Aimee's establishment with distain in her tone. It was clear she didn't approve of her daughter's chosen vocation. He thought of the crucifix affixed to the wall and smiled. Aimee must've been a terror to her mother growing up. How had she gone from being a good Catholic girl to a seller of sin?

"Do you really believe she has no idea what her sister did while on the premises?"

Darryl shrugged. "I'm sure she has an idea, but even I don't like thinking about my siblings' sex lives."

He followed Darryl into the bull pen that housed the DU—Detective Unit. Only five of the ten desks were occupied. James eased himself into the closest vacant desk, claiming it as his own, before surveying the small space, noting two open interview rooms, a kitchenette, and a large conference room. Each contained the same charcoal grey industrial carpet and cream coloured walls.

The parking lot was visible through the large bank of windows behind Inspector Donovan's desk and the sunlight streamed in, despite the late hour, bringing with it the oppressive heat that was barely kept at bay by the ancient air conditioner that circulated stale, semi-cool air. James released a couple buttons of his shirt and rolled up his sleeves as Darryl disappeared down the hall toward the toilets.

Amelia Donovan, her phone pressed to her ear, closed her desk drawer with too much strength. Coffee sloshed over the side of her mug and spilled over some documents. She cursed savagely then apologised to the person on the other end of the phone. His eyebrow rose at her extensive vocabulary. He sensed he shouldn't cross her, and not just because she'd be his boss in a couple months. She had an attitude that warned others not to fuck with her, but Darryl also told him she was fiercely loyal to those she considered family, and that there was no use arguing with her. She made a mule look cooperative.

He turned on his computer. So far, it had been a hectic first day but he was loving every minute of it—except the dead woman. He didn't like that one damn bit. He let out a deep breath, hoping to ease some of the tension from his body. No cop liked to see a young life cut short.

He leaned back in his chair and reviewed the case, his mind replaying each moment since the discovery of the body. It had been a vicious attack. Despite Ruth Burnes's adamant denial, someone out there hadn't liked Louisa and whoever it was had known she'd be walking alone late at night. Who else besides Ruth and Aimee—with the exception of Aimee's employees—had known Louisa frequented her sister's club? The list was bound to be short, which made him wonder if they hadn't already closed in on the suspect.

His mind flashed on Aimee and the gentle sway of her hips. He'd been hard from the moment he'd caught sight of her lace bra playing peek-a-boo beneath her blouse. It had made the interview difficult. He was thankful Darryl had been there to keep him from saying or doing something stupid.

Yes, Aimee was sexy. But she was also his victim's sister and as much as he'd like to discount her as a suspect, he didn't have enough proof to convince himself that she was innocent of any wrongdoing. One thing was for sure, he was attracted to her. And it was a really bad idea to entertain any thoughts about her. Too bad he couldn't stop the fantasies from crossing his mind. He cursed silently, knowing he'd been too long without a woman.

He reached up and ran his hand over his face in an effort to erase the fatigue, and felt his crooked nose beneath his palm. His nose had been broken one too many times in his youth when his bone structure was still changing and had never healed properly. He always played a rough game of rugby and didn't like to lose. He had the same attitude about life in general.

Darryl returned to his desk wearing a suave suit that must've had him roasting beneath it. He was freshly shaved and James caught the subtle cologne he wore.

Male voices filled the room as two men exited the elevator and started toward them. James studied them as their long legs ate up the space and with each step brought them closer. The man on the left had dark blond hair and brown eyes and wore a scowl on his face, the complete opposite of the grinning man beside him with cornflower blue eyes and black hair. Both men walked with confidence but the man on the left held himself more rigidly and James figured he must have some military background—something he'd also noted in his partner.

The dark haired man let out a wolf whistle. "Shit, Hill, you look like you're going to a wedding. What's the occasion?"

Darryl glared. "If you must know, I'm taking my wife to dinner."

"I guess you're not talking Tanner's Steak and Grill?"

"No." He adjusted his tie. "It's our six-month anniversary."

"Hey, you getting in on this or what?" the dark haired man asked Amelia, whose desk was the closest to him.

She glared at him. "I'm on a personal call."

He stared at her in shock. "Who knew Donovan had more than one friend?" he asked his colleagues before turning to Darryl. "Hey, does Kellie know Donovan's cheating on her?"

Amelia picked up a stress ball from her desk and pitched it with deadly accuracy, hitting the man square in the chest.

"*Ow.*" He rubbed his chest where the ball had hit. The blond reached down and retrieved it, opened his desk drawer, and dropped it in.

"I'm sorry, Megan, go on," Amelia said into the phone, then turned her chair so her back was to them.

"Matthews, Doyle, meet James Hawke, the new recruit. James, this is Dean Matthews and Nicholas Doyle."

He rose from his seat and shook each of the men's hands. Darryl had given him a quick rundown on the team on the drive over. Darryl had recently married and his wife, Kellie, worked at the LAC in SCIA—Special Crimes and Internal Affairs—up on the top floor of the building. He was the newest to the group and had been working in Harbour Bay going on four years.

Dean Matthews was quiet, a hard man to get to know, and he seemed to favour a horrible selection of pastel and floral button-up shirts.

While the rest of his teammates had serious temperaments, Nicholas Doyle was the jovial one who kept things light. While women tended to fawn all over him, he wasn't a player. The only son in a family of five, he spent his free time in the gym downstairs teaching self-defence.

"Welcome to the team," Nick said, leaning against his desk. "I'm sure you'll fit right in. I hear you've got a DB."

"Yeah. Stabbing victim." He stilled as a blonde dressed in a dark midnight blue strapless ankle length dress stepped out of the elevator. Her hair was curled and artfully arranged, cascading down her back.

Nick followed his gaze. "Wow, Kellie, you look gorgeous."

"Put your tongue back in your head, Doyle," Darryl warned, placing his hands on his wife's small waist and leaning in to kiss her. What would it be like to love someone as much as Darryl clearly loved his wife? "I've got my mobile, but if you ring me, you'd better be dying," Darryl said, and gently pushed on Kellie's back to get her moving. "I'll see you all in the morning."

"If you can move," Nick said, and Darryl and Kellie shared a private smile.

Amelia returned Kellie's wave before saying goodbye to the person on the other end of the phone. James could tell Nick was itching to ask her all about the mysterious woman but Amelia gave him one look that dampened his enthusiasm.

James hid his smile. Despite the different personalities, everyone in the office seemed to get along well, and he could feel the camaraderie between them. He hoped he would be a part of it one day.

After Kellie and Darryl left, Amelia stood and hooked her holster to her belt. She glanced over at him and asked if he wanted to continue the line of questioning of those involved in Louisa Burnes's life or search through her office, apartment, and car—which they'd found parked a block away from where she had been murdered.

"I'll stay here and do some follow-up questions. See if I can build a timeline. Do you need me to do anything while I'm stuck here?"

"There's a few reports that need typing up," she said.

He nodded. "I'm on it."

She shot him a look of surprise that slowly morphed into a smile. She gave a brief nod of thanks before saying, "I'll see you ladies in the morning."

A moment later, the elevator doors were closing behind her.

He located the files Darryl had uploaded earlier with the names and addresses of those involved in the case.

Nick stretched. "Okay, who wants coffee? It's going to be a long night."

Dean grunted. Nick seemed to take that as an affirmative. James sent an uneasy glance toward the break room and thought of the congealed gunk in the bottom of the carafe he'd seen earlier.

Back home, their only female officer always made sure the coffee pot was clean and contained hot coffee all day long. Would Detective Donovan do the same? He doubted it. She didn't seem the type. The other woman he'd worked with had been a real mother hen, a part-timer who always went home at two-thirty to pick her kids up from school and make dinner for her husband.

"Not that crap," Nick said, following James's gaze. "I like having tastebuds. I'm going for the proper stuff."

"Sure, if you don't mind." He shifted in his seat to pull his wallet from his back pocket.

Nick waved his hand. "No, it's all good, I've got you. Next time, you can buy."

"Deal."

Chapter 6

Amelia Donovan unlocked the door to Louisa Burnes's apartment. The place was clean, almost to the point of compulsive. Everything had its place, neatly organised in the two-bedroom dwelling. The garbage had been taken out so the room smelled of nothing but the perfume ornament sitting on Louisa's side table, set to emit the scent of rose every half hour.

The blinds were open, allowing the last of the day's light to brighten the open area. On the east side of the room stood an oak bookcase filled with law volumes and romance books. She got the sense Louisa had no social life.

Amelia snapped on a pair of white latex gloves and sifted through the stack of mail resting on the clean marble kitchen counter. All she found were bills and bank statements, which showed less than frivolous spending. It appeared the victim didn't know how to have fun. She spent her money on expensive clothes, her hair, nails, and her books and not much else. Except perhaps Club X.

Amelia moved around the room, stopping to take photos or to open a drawer or cabinet. There was nothing so far that hinted at a reason to want Louisa dead. Unless being a clean freak was a motive.

She found the bed made, the sheets tucked in under the mattress, not just pulled up, and the pillows fluffed. She doubted whether they would find any bodily fluids on the sheets with the exception of the victim's but she tended to go elsewhere for that. Everything she had found so far had led her to believe that the victim was a solitary person, that she didn't like sharing her haven with anyone.

The apartment reminded Amelia of her own place, devoid of colour and sentiment. The only difference was the price range. Louisa preferred labels whereas Amelia had an eclectic range of garage sale items. She also wasn't as anal as Louisa Burnes but she was close enough. Every morning, she made her bed, took the garbage out, and made sure that if she didn't come home there was nothing she didn't want anyone to see. After seeing so many victims' houses and learning how they lived, she never wanted anyone making judgements about the way she chose to live her life.

Amelia opened the bathroom cabinet and found a mass of cleaning and medical supplies and a variety of different brands of moisturiser, nail polish, and make-up removers as if Louisa couldn't figure which one she liked best. Amelia flicked through the tubes of anti-inflammatory creams and boxes of Panadol and Strepsils. She didn't find any condoms in any of the drawers in the bedroom nor the bathroom but she did uncover Louisa's birth control pills.

Louisa may have been having sex, but she never brought anyone home. Amelia found no evidence of a male in the apartment nor any clothing left behind from any previous sexual partners. Amelia knew that if any man stayed the night often enough, they always ended up leaving something behind, like socks or shirts. Once, a man had left his underwear at Amelia's place. How he managed that, she wasn't sure, and always found herself collecting a pile of discarded clothes which she washed and took to the Salvation Army once the man had left her life.

She found no hints of close friends in Louisa's home, her address book showing only a few names and numbers. The only photos around the apartment were childhood shots taken of her and Aimee.

The prints on the walls displayed exotic places around the world—Egypt, Paris, Venice—the usual selection that romantics wished to visit. Amelia found herself wondering why Louisa never went. It wasn't due to lack of money, that was for sure. Even after paying off her car, apartment, and expensive medical bills for her mother's treatments, she still had more than enough to bankroll an extended trip around Europe. She would mention this when she returned to the LAC for Hill or Hawke to follow up on.

Amelia packed up her things and resealed the apartment. There might be times they would need to return so they couldn't as yet release Louisa's home to the family. She made her way to the lift inside the complex. She still had the office and car to go through, then her own set of questions to ask.

Chapter 7

The funeral was a solemn affair. The Harbour Bay Catholic Church was filled with all of Ruth's friends—her coven, as Aimee had always called the ladies from church—who had turned out to support her in her time of need, offering her sympathy at the loss of a beloved daughter.

What a crock of shit.

The pious priest read out his sermon, commending Louisa for her many virtues. In the Burnes household, it had always been that way. Louisa could do no wrong. When they had been young, Louisa had gotten her into trouble more times than she could count and not once had Ruth believed her younger daughter when she had vehemently denied any involvement.

Biting her lip kept her from laughing out loud. The priest wouldn't know her sister from Eve, and yet, he still felt the need to believe her in a better place up in Heaven with their Father, the Lord. If only the dear man spouting off how wonderful she'd been knew the truth, that she'd spent her nights at Club X. He—along with everyone else inside the church—would have had a coronary if they knew.

She pretended not to notice the stares and looks of shock from the so-called mourners. They all knew what she did for a living—or had heard several unsavoury things about her, which she guessed were probably all true—and they all disapproved. Had it been a couple hundred years ago, knowing these lovely old ladies, Aimee would've been stoned or burned to death for her choices. Not that she would ever change a thing.

During her rebellious teenager years, she had done everything to put her mother in an early grave, even going as far as to show up at this very church, dressed up as a Goth with one of her many boyfriends who had owned a motorcycle, had chains around his neck, an eyebrow piercing and several lewd tattoos. She had caused quite a stir and had greatly shamed her mother, which had been the point.

She'd been the talk of church lunches for months to come, only hearing about it from her sister, since Ruth had forbidden her to join them—ever again. Finding her mother's stress point sent her on a merry bender. She'd been desperate for her mother's attention, no matter the form it came in. Years later, after several margaritas, Louisa had confessed she had envied Aimee for her freedom.

That had been the first time she'd understood Louisa hadn't wanted to be their mother's favourite, the good girl, and that maybe she had wanted to break free, too. In the past few years, her sister had thoroughly enjoyed herself.

Aimee stood alone at the funeral, off to the side, away from prying eyes and clammy hands—away from fake sympathy. Half the people there were curious bystanders. Her sister's murder had been sensationalised on the front page of the Harbour Bay Tribute, drawing all the morbid individuals out of the woodwork. Reporters had hounded her and the club since the article went to print asking for her take on the matter. Like she would want to comment on her own sister's murder. She may be low but she wasn't *that* low. They had also asked if there was any correlation between the murder and her sex club.

Nausea rose in her throat. She swallowed the foul taste. It was a reasonable question, one she wasn't sure she wanted the answer to. Tears pricked her eyes but she refused to let them fall. She would not give anyone any satisfaction or juicy titbit to tell. She would mourn properly, in private.

Cold and disjointed from reality, Aimee tried to understand how this could be happening. She should've taken the time to get more involved in her sister's life. Louisa had almost been like a stranger to her over the years and she admitted she'd never tried for a more familiar relationship. In her youth, she had felt betrayed by both her sister and mother. However, it had been easy to forgive Louisa for following her mother's demands.

Now she would never get the chance to enjoy having a sister, one she could share her most valuable secrets with. She had missed that growing up, having left home at sixteen only to return five years later to the same reception she received when she'd departed.

Louisa had made an effort to mend the rift their mother had caused but what had been done was not easily undone. It had taken some time for Aimee to allow Louisa back into her life, her heart cold, so she wouldn't be hurt again by those who were supposed to love her.

Her skin burned where the sun's harsh rays made contact as she followed behind the rest of the congregation as they moved toward the cemetery beyond the church. Her sister's coffin was lowered. Her mother had dressed Louisa in some shapeless virginal white Sunday dress, as if her style of clothing would guarantee her a spot in Heaven. Her blonde hair was stylishly curled and pearls adorned her throat. She wore basic make-up just to add colour to her dead skin and she had a pair of white flats that looked like tennis shoes on her feet. That had been the last straw for Aimee. Her mother hadn't known Louisa any more than the priest had.

If Louisa weren't already dead, she would have died looking at herself now. She had worn nothing but stilettos, her wardrobe filled with expensive labels like Gucci and Versace. She wore Chanel No. 5 perfume and bought her cosmetics from David Jones.

Aimee's gaze swept the cemetery as white roses were thrown on the coffin. She found the two detectives, Hawke and Hill, blending into the mob of funeral goers, both dressed in black suits. The younger one, Hawke, nodded when he met her gaze. She offered him a weak smile as Amazing Grace began to play.

The breeze was hot and dry, just another Australian summer. Aimee turned and started moving away from the grave site, but didn't move fast enough. Her mother intercepted her.

"Aimee," Ruth said coldly, casting her disapproving gaze over her, frowning at what she saw.

Aimee wore a simple black dress that covered her cleavage and fell to her knees demurely, her make-up and jewellery understated, yet she knew her mother found fault with her—as always. She was sure her mother wished it was her in the grave instead of Louisa.

She narrowed her eyes, wondering if her mother had ever loved her. "Mother, how are you?"

Ruth dabbed at her eyes with a handkerchief. "My beloved daughter is dead, murdered. How do you think I'm doing?"

She shrugged. Her mother was extremely self-centred, and all she could see was how she was affected. No one else mattered.

"I was just being polite," Aimee said. "I don't much care how you feel. Louisa's the one I feel for. I can only imagine what she went through that night. How she must've suffered. How alone she was. No one should be alone when they die."

Ruth pinned her with a hard glare, a look that once made her quiver in fear. Now it only served as a reminder of why she avoided her mother.

"Have you spoken to the police yet?" Ruth asked.

Aimee's gaze went to the two detectives leaning

against a regulation red Holden SS Commodore. "We've had words."

"Really, Aimee, your sister was just murdered, how can you act so flippantly?"

"Well, Mother, it's my way of dealing. I don't have anyone I can turn to. Plus, I'm still getting over the shock of hearing about Lou. I'm sure I must have missed your call."

Ruth didn't apologise. "I didn't call you."

She'd already known that. Not that she would have knowingly taken a call from her mother but she had checked for missed calls and voicemails.

"So you thought it'd be best if the police told me?" Hands on hips, she glared at her. She really didn't understand this woman who had given her life.

"I thought you'd find out sooner or later. No use wasting your time with a phone call. I know you're a busy woman." She sneered.

"Well, thank you, Mother," she said sarcastically. "It's just the kind of news I want complete strangers to tell me. But then again, it would be just the same if you'd called me."

Ruth let out a deep breath. "Aimee, you're being unreasonable."

She snorted. "Of course, it's always me, isn't it, Mother?"

She didn't wait for an answer, continuing toward the detectives instead. Detective Hill pushed away from the car when he saw her start in their direction. A second later, Hawke did the same.

"Detectives, how nice to see you again. I thought I'd answered all your questions. Do you have more?" Aimee asked, crossing her arms protectively. Her sister's murder had put her on edge and muted her usually outgoing nature.

"Not at this time, Ms. Burnes. It's protocol in all homicide cases that we monitor the funeral. Just in case the suspect shows himself," Detective Hill said.

"We've found that most perpetrators will return to admire their work," Detective Hawke added.

Aimee turned back at the hovering, ghoulish spectators. "I'm afraid you've wasted your time, boys. I can assure you that each of those so-called mourners are not killers. Their motives for being here may not be completely honourable, but I've known those judgemental bitch—ladies—all my life," she said, not wanting to sound overly harsh.

"How are you doing?" Detective Hill asked.

Aimee shifted her feet, her two-inch heels sinking into the lush green lawn. "I've had better days."

The two detectives nodded. Beyond them, the gathering had begun to disperse, the festivities over and the real party—the free food and drink at the reception—was about to begin. Detective Hill appeared to focus on something over her shoulder and Aimee followed his gaze, staring daggers at the retreating form of her mother.

She certainly played this for all it was worth.

Not that she doubted her mother was mourning the loss of her favoured daughter, but Ruth's empathy could only go so far.

Over the years, Aimee had only seen her mother upset a handful of times. Angry or disappointed, most definitely, but not even after her father had left them did Ruth shed a tear.

Interesting. Maybe the old bitch had loved Louisa more than Aimee thought. Although, had it been her in that grave instead of Louisa, her mother probably wouldn't have attended.

The thought dampened her already low spirits.

"Have there been any developments?" she asked, trying to distract herself from the cold, harsh reality of her relationship with her mother and focusing on the more tragic circumstances of her sister's death.

"It's still a work in progress," Detective Hill said. "Early stages. Unfortunately, at this time, we've nothing to report. We will need to speak with your employees, Ms. Burnes. Are you able to arrange it?"

"Of course. May I ask why?"

"It would be of great help if we could piece together a more thorough timeline. Perhaps one of them spoke with your sister and might be able to shed some light on her personal life. We've discovered precious little and could use some help."

She swallowed at the lump in her throat. She should've been able to give the detectives what they needed to close the case. Instead, her stubbornness had kept her at arm's length from Louisa. Something she'd regret for the rest of her life.

Aimee nodded. "Tomorrow night at eleven the club is hosting a mixer for our clients. All my employees will be there. It's something we do every month. I'll organise it so you'll have a chance to speak with each of them."

"Thank you, Ms. Burnes."

She smiled but knew it failed to reach her eyes. "Please call me Aimee."

Detective Hill nodded. "I apologise for monopolising your time. Please go be with your family."

Aimee bit her lower lip. "Actually, you were my excuse for escape. My mother is a deeply religious woman as I'm sure you're aware, with antiquated beliefs and an unreasonable desire to have us follow them. She never learned that stuffing her values down our throats was not the way to go."

"I'm sorry."

"As am I. For many things, the least of which is my lack of relationship with my mother. I'll leave you to your suspect watching, but I hope you take what I said into consideration. The worst these old biddies would've done is recite a bible verse or condemn Louisa to eternal damnation. I know they've done so to me in the past. But they aren't the type to stab a woman."

Unless it was in the back.

"Noted," Detective Hill said.

"But you have a job to do. I wish you luck. Louisa deserved better than to be left like garbage in an alley." A tear rolled down her cheek. If anyone deserved to end up discarded it was Aimee, who'd never done a decent thing in her life.

"I promise you, Ms. Burnes, we'll find the person responsible and get justice for your sister," Detective Hawke said.

Aimee was touched by his tone. It had been a long time since a man had promised her anything. The last one who'd made a promise had cost her everything. Was James Hawke as sincere as he sounded?

He was certainly handsome, and his velvety voice was enough to send shivers down her spine. His dark suit fit snugly over his wide shoulders and broad chest. She could imagine her nails digging into his flesh in the height of passion. As she did with most men she met, Aimee wondered what he'd be like in bed. Tender and caring, no doubt. He seemed the type to tend to his partner's needs before his own. She shivered with carnal delight then silently cursed herself. She couldn't believe she was lusting over a man at her sister's funeral. She really was the worst type of person. But then she shouldn't be surprised at herself.

"Thank you, Detective Hawke, Detective Hill. I appreciate your dedication." She shook both men's hands, her fingers tingling when James's larger hand wrapped around her own. Aimee could've sworn she stopped breathing.

She glanced up from beneath her lashes to gauge his response. The face she thought so open appeared carved from granite. She felt the tug of disappointment. What had she been expecting— desire for her written on his face? If she was honest with herself, then yes. It was no more than any other man had done in her presence.

"I hope you find the person responsible," she said. "Louisa deserves justice. I never appreciated her in life. It is all I can hope for in death. Again, please let me know if I can help in anyway."

Aimee started towards the parking lot where her black Honda CR-V was parked. As she wept, she was thankful no one could see her. She hated public displays and right now she was close to losing it. She slipped inside her car and jammed the key in the ignition before she began to sob and choked back her despair, resting her forehead against the steering wheel.

If only she could go back in time. There was so much she'd change about the past. Now it was too late. She took a calming breath, unable to understand why her sister was gone. It was such a senseless crime. Had her club been responsible as the reporter had suggested? Had she inadvertently painted a target on Lou's back by allowing her entry into the club?

Guilt ate at her until she could hardly breathe. She'd done some horrible things in her life, made many wrong choices, but introducing her sister into her world was the worst. Even if it had nothing to do with her death, she'd still set Louisa on her path of self-destruction. Whatever the reason, someone had decided to rid the world of her, and Aimee knew she was involved somehow.

Chapter 8

James's gaze followed Aimee. This time it wasn't her enticing walk capturing his attention but her straight back and stiff shoulders. He saw her pain acutely, an aura of sorrow and grief that wafted around her. Had she cried? He doubted it. She seemed the type who'd fight the emotion, believing it made her weak and probably vulnerable. Aimee had already proven she could push aside her feelings, refusing to display them to an audience. But he figured when she did it would slice her to the bone and leave her exposed and raw.

"She's having a hard time," Darryl said. "I can imagine her pain. I have two brothers. I'm the middle child. Both serve overseas. They've had a few close calls over the years and given me a couple of hard knocks. Thankfully, never lost one though."

But just how much was her own doing? Guilt had a way of consuming a person.

He wondered if that was why she was being so accommodating. Not many people, including the innocent, were so helpful. There was always something they wanted to hide that they believed would ruin their lives if it got out, but Aimee Burnes genuinely appeared to want to catch her sister's killer and didn't care for embarrassment or consequences to herself.

He tucked his hands into his pockets. "I suppose she's right about this being a waste of our time."

"Probably, but you never know where the most valuable information will come from and it's our duty to explore all avenues."

He followed his partner into the church. A table had been set by the open door filled with small triangular sandwiches and a variety of non-alcoholic beverages. A medium sized fan circulated the warm air around the room. Sweat rolled down his back and dampened the fabric.

He found it strange none of the mourners were Louisa's age. None of the guests he and Darryl spoke to had seen her except in passing since she was sixteen. He doubted if any of them even remembered her. They spoke of her in simple terms. Sweet. Caring. Dutiful. Unlike Aimee, who they all knew with vivid detail. The harlot. The strumpet. The bane of Ruth's existence.

Not one indiscretion had been missed, and he and Darryl were regaled with story after story of Aimee's many disappointments and perceived sins. James had to cough to cover the laughter he barely contained a couple times. Aimee sure knew what pushed her mother's buttons. James would've loved to meet sixteen-year-old Aimee. They would've had a lot of fun together. Hell, they still could. But he was sure *that* Aimee was gone; judgement and recriminations had chipped away at her free spirit.

Not that she wasn't interesting now. He was more than a little curious. Aimee had become stronger, more sexual, and had a wealth of knowledge behind her grey eyes.

Darryl cleared his throat as yet another of Ruth's friends departed. "With this crowd, was it any wonder she rebelled?"

He agreed. He hailed from a small town but he'd never had to put up with the kind of scrutiny Aimee and Louisa had lived under. He cast his gaze in Ruth's direction, where she sat amongst her friends, leaning on them. He tried not to be judgmental but when there was a loss, family were supposed to band together and lend support. Ruth should be sharing her grief with her remaining daughter, providing comfort.

He didn't know what happened to cause the rift between them, other than her antics years before, but Aimee's comments said there was no chance of a reconciliation. A shame. For some reason he had an idea Aimee could really use forgiveness and love right now.

He leaned against the nearby wall and studied the small gathering.

"We haven't learned anything except they all believe Ms. Burnes capable of murder," he said when Darryl moved to stand beside him. "It's a good thing they're not on the jury. They'd have her hung, drawn, and quartered before dawn."

"Not a forgiving lot, are they?"

He snorted. That was an understatement. These ladies were the most judgmental people he'd ever met, and not one appeared to look for the kindness in Aimee. She may not have their acceptance, but she was certainly a topic of conversation.

"Let's head out. We've learned all that we're going to."

No argument from him. Despite supposedly being in mourning for the young woman's life, women sat around gossiping and condemning the deceased's sister. Aimee deserved better.

He wasn't sure why he had a burning desire to defend her. He sensed there was more beneath that gorgeous exterior…a tender heart that needed protecting.

Chapter 9

James followed Darryl inside Club X and towards the podium where they'd first met Aimee a couple of days ago. She wasn't there and in her place were two women, welcoming their clients into the club. His eyebrow rose as he took in their appearance. They wore outfits that bared a lot of skin, which would have him arresting them for indecent exposure should they leave the club without first covering up.

"Hi, and welcome to Club X," the first woman said, her voice a poor imitation of Aimee's husky tone. She was trying too hard to be sexy.

The other woman held a tray of shot glasses filled with bright blue alcohol and offered them each a drink. Both declined.

"Aimee Burnes?" Darryl asked, as he held up his official I.D. The two women shared a brief glance.

"In there," the first woman said, pointing to the right, toward the adjoining room and bar. He noticed her voice changed, gone was her attempt at a sultry timbre.

He slipped inside the room, blinking as his eyes adjusted to the darker light that provided an air of anonymity and mystery to what should have felt seedy and degrading. Aimee sure knew how to put her clients at ease. From the décor, he could easily believe he was at a nightclub and not a high-end bordello.

He had led a rather quiet life, he reflected, never once entering a sex club. Not even on an official capacity. Come to think of it, he'd never entered a sex shop before, either. Toys and fetishes didn't interest him. He reached the bar and searched the faces for Aimee, silently cursing his stupidity. If only he could say it was purely professional reasons that had him eagerly awaiting the stunningly beautiful and undeniably seductive woman, but he knew he'd be lying. He'd been completely blown away by his desire toward her, his traitorous body yearning for her, and he couldn't seem to get it under control.

The man beside him vacated a stool and he slipped onto it while Darryl leaned his hips casually against the bar.

The room was hot and James had already began to sweat. Beyond the mass of people was a stage almost hidden in the billowing smoke surrounding the floor, swirling around the partygoers knees, wafting higher, enveloping the entire room. Several support beams rose from the stage and connected with the ceiling.

The low lights in the room dimmed until he could barely see the outline of the people surrounding him. A spotlight hit the stage and the music changed. Aimee, dressed in a cheeky schoolgirl's uniform complete with short tartan mini skirt and knee length socks, stepped out. She was followed by ten buff men who looked like they spent their entire lives in the gym. Their golden skin was oiled so they shined in the bright beam that highlighted them.

Her body moved with the beat to the music, her men copying her movements as she sashayed across the stage. Her hips moved up and down in rhythm, her eyes sparkling. She was enjoying herself as much as her audience was. Darryl shifted beside him, and James felt grateful that he wasn't the only one effected by the sultry dance.

The short skirt twirled as she spun around, offering a tantalising view of red underwear. Her long legs looked supple and soft and all he could think about was having them wrapped around his waist. She would be a creative lover, her movements sensual, and he imagined her repeating them in a more private setting.

His mind flashed to the funeral the day before. She'd worn a simple black dress, the cut not overtly sexy, but there was no denying the body beneath the fabric. For a brief moment, he hadn't recognised her. Her face had been made-up in nude tones, so unlike the dark smoky eyes and blood red lips he'd come to realise was her usual.

She'd been different then. Close to tears, yet gallantly trying to hold them at bay. He couldn't work her out. One minute, she had seemed lost and vulnerable and in the next her backbone was made of steel once more. She was clearly grieving yet refused to show any weakness. Which woman was the real one and which was the façade?

She leaned back as if in reckless abandon, her high breasts pushing at the confines of her tight white blouse. The tops of the creamy globes threatened to spill over a naughty vibrant red lace bra that matched her lipstick and underwear. She grabbed the supporting column behind her with her left hand as her right hand slowly made a descent from those full kissable lips, down her delicate throat and chest as her heart shaped bottom moved toward the floor, using the pole to support her back until her arse was kissing the three-inch heels that sparkled like diamonds in the spotlight.

She ran her hand enticingly over her breast, then down her taut stomach to rest on her thigh. She licked her lips in a way that would send every male in the room hard and straining for release. He was amazed a riot hadn't broken out. Aimee drew his attention once more as she reversed the process, her hand and body moving upwards, following the same path.

Wolf whistles and screams of enthusiasm from both males and females shocked him. He was used to keeping sex confined to the bedroom and never before had he seen such a public display. The lust around him was palpable—almost as thick as the smoke surrounding his knees—and he could hear gasps as Aimee grabbed hold of the pole at the top with both hands and winked at the crowd.

She lifted herself up and wrapped her thighs around the pole near her hands, clamping her strong muscles to hold herself up as she released her hands from the pole. She hung upside down, her hair draping down toward the floor in waves of rich chestnut.

This was certainly a woman who knew how to use what she'd been given. Her movements and seductive looks had everyone in the room mesmerised. Even he was drawn into her web. Every look, every touch and muscle flex had been choreographed to get the most reaction, and it was working.

Aimee slid down the pole much to the pleasure of the male contingent. She flipped her legs, once more upright, and made her way, hips pronounced, back to the men dancing provocatively on stage. She ran one index finger down a ripped and toned six-pack before placing it in her mouth. As she turned to the crowd, she sucked briefly on her finger.

She turned back to the man and slowly moved down his body, manicured nails scraping his golden skin. The man's stomach bunched beneath her fingers as her nails tickled him. He didn't envy his job and wondered what the man was thinking to ensure he remained soft. He knew nothing would stop *him* from saluting the ceiling had he been the one on stage.

Aimee reached his muscled thighs. Were they were sleeping together? Surely, no two people could set a blaze like that and not have a yearning to put it out later, or maybe that was what this night was about. Any woman in this room would've been honoured to ride off into the night with the man on stage, who at that very moment grabbed Aimee's hands, his muscles bulging and straining, and pulled her up, jerking her off her feet before her creamy legs wrapped around his trim waist.

He held her hands high above her head, her breasts in line with his lips as he bent his head forward as if not touching her would be a crime. James swallowed hard. Excitement bristled in the air. His eyes narrowed as those lips neared Aimee's breasts, but to his relief, stopped a mere breath from touching.

A collective groan escaped many of the onlookers, and James fought not to ask himself why the man touching Aimee bothered him. He barely knew her, certainly had no hold or sway over her. He may want her. But he'd never been possessive over a woman before and certainly didn't like the fact that this woman brought out that emotion in him.

Her stiletto-heeled feet touched the stage once more as the music died down and she was rewarded with applause. Perspiration coated her forehead from the exertion and heat of the spotlight. She blinked into the crowd, obviously blinded by the harsh light as she spoke loudly.

"Thank you. I would like to welcome you all to Club X. I hope you have a wonderful time and come back soon. Enjoy yourselves," she said, her tone tantalising.

She jumped off the stage as her male dancers continued to gyrate on stage, her once captive audience breaking up, finding themselves a partner for the night. Aimee mingled with the crowd, speaking to a few of her clients before spotting him.

Her gaze locked on his as she moved toward him. A tingle of awareness darted through him, just as it had the day of the funeral when she'd shaken his hand. He fought against showing her how much she affected him.

A dazzling smile stretched her mouth as she approached. "Detectives, good to see you."

"Ms. Burnes," Darryl said, his tone professional as if he hadn't been affected by her sultry display on stage.

James wasn't so cool and quickly shielded his body beneath the cover of the bar before anyone noticed.

"I assume you want to get straight to work?" she asked. Did she feel any of the attraction he fought against?

Darryl nodded. "If you wouldn't mind."

Before he'd finished speaking, a tall blonde with Scandinavian features appeared behind Aimee and her mesmerising blue eyes winked at them as she placed her arm around her boss's shoulders.

Aimee didn't even glance behind her to see who was hanging off her. Was she so used to be grabbed and touched that she had learned not to care, and why was he so concerned? It shouldn't matter to him who touched her or where. Yet, for some reason, it did.

"This is Tiffany Myers. She said she'll go first," Aimee said.

"Hi," Tiffany said, and James remembered her from the day he and Darryl had notified Aimee of her sister's death. He greeted her before his gaze returned to Aimee.

"I'm going to go mingle," she said. "Let me know if you need anything. Please help yourself to some drinks."

Darryl stared at her as if she was attempting to corrupt him. "We're on duty," he replied.

Aimee raised an eyebrow. "Don't look at me like I'm trying to lure you over to the dark side, Detective Hill. I was simply offering you a beverage. We do serve non-alcoholic drinks here. Besides, I have no interest in enticing married men." She glanced down at his wedding ring. "I know I wouldn't appreciate some woman persuading my husband to stray."

Darryl sent her a wry smile. "My wife will be happy to hear that. She won't need to sharpen her claws."

Aimee laughed. "I think I'd like to meet your wife, Detective Hill. She sounds like someone I'd like very much."

She disappeared into the crowd and his gaze followed her. He frowned and stared at the dark stained wood of the bar, hoping his interest had gone unnoticed. He had to be more careful. If Darryl suspected, he'd pull him from the case so fast his head would spin. And he'd be right. He certainly couldn't investigate the case properly if he was distracted by a person of interest—and that was exactly what Aimee was. She might have said the right things so far, but she had yet to be vindicated.

"So, which one of you cuties will be interrogating me?" Tiffany asked, as if the interrogation would be a spa treatment and massage.

Darryl let out a long sigh. "We should split up.

Cover twice the ground."

He nodded and carefully stood, hoping that the remainder of his hard-on wasn't visible, relieved at the low lighting. "Right."

He turned away and walked toward a woman in a sexy red negligee. How the hell was he going to get through the night?

Then he reminded himself Darryl was a man, too, and was no less turned on by what was going on around them. Unlike Darryl, James didn't have a wife at home he loved dearly.

Suck it up, man.

He smiled at Aimee's employee, displaying his brand new Harbour Bay police I.D.

Jenna Carpenter—Miss Red Negligee—checked him out and asked if he'd brought handcuffs. He bit back a groan.

It was going to be a long and painful night.

Chapter 10

Darryl directed Tiffany outside the main event room and into the foyer where the two women were still welcoming a few stragglers into the building, clearly offering themselves as much as the drinks with their body language and sultry expressions.

Aimee must make a killing.

He stopped where they wouldn't be overheard, but could still see if anyone approached.

The blonde waited patiently, and Darryl frowned at the fact she was so eager to be interrogated. She wore next to nothing, her small strapless dress clinging to her youthful body like a second skin, outlining her amazing assets.

"So, Aimee says I'm to tell you the truth, no matter what I'm asked," Tiffany said, as if she thought he wouldn't believe her otherwise. She twirled a lock of blonde hair around her index finger and he imagined her popping bubble gum in her mouth.

"That's very kind of her," he said.

Tiffany nodded. "I know what guys like you

think of places like this, but Club X is a safe place and a great environment to work in."

She was one of those. An eternal optimist who saw the best in every situation. The type who would find herself in trouble when she undoubtedly trusted the wrong person.

How did a girl like her end up in a place like this? She didn't appear to be any older than twenty-one. His mind ran through possibilities. She was probably still in school and only worked here to pay her fees. At least he hoped.

"So tell me about Aimee," he said. He was already regretting agreeing to take Tiffany while James went off and found another employee. Her voice grated on his nerves like the proverbial fingernail to the chalkboard.

Tiffany smiled. "She's wonderful. Kind and caring. She's an awesome boss."

"What about her relationship with her sister?"

She frowned and chewed on her bottom lip. "I'm not sure how to answer. I don't want to betray her confidence."

"Tiffany, Aimee did say for you to tell the truth, remember?"

She nodded and let out a deep breath. "Aimee told me she felt like she could never measure up. Louisa was the perfect child. Aimee could never make her mother proud and I know it hurt her. She likes to pretend she can't feel, but I know it's not true. She feels too much."

"I got the sense she and Ruth don't get along," he said, thinking back to the funeral and how Aimee hadn't consoled her mother, nor had Ruth reached out to comfort her only remaining daughter. He'd thought it odd at the time, but he hadn't spoken to either of his brothers in a while. The eldest, Jack, had a son he hadn't seen since his birth. Now he was curious over the lack of feeling between the two women.

"Aimee tries to stay away as much as possible," Tiffany said. "Their relationship is strained. Aimee once told me that when she was sixteen she had this boyfriend who pressured her into having…well, you know."

He raised an eyebrow, unable to wrap his head around the fact that a girl who worked in a sex club couldn't say the word sex.

What the hell did she do around the place?

"After which, he dumped her," Tiffany continued. "Typical man. And you know what? Her mother couldn't even offer support. How lame is that? All she said was, 'Well, what did you expect?' What a B-I-T-C-H."

Tiffany leaned closer and dropped her voice to a whisper. "Her mum's not very pleased with her. Can you imagine a daughter of a Catholic woman owning sex club?" Blushing, she gave a smile at the irony before explaining how she knew. "I overhead Aimee and Louisa talking one day. Their mum's sick. She's got some kind of a blood disease. She's being treated but they say it's only a matter of time and Louisa wanted them to make up and let bygones be bygones."

He indicated that he understood, and for some reason felt like he was gossiping. It was a strange feeling, but talking to this girl made him feel like putting on pyjamas and ordering pizza. He took a deep breath as he lined up the next question.

"So Aimee was jealous of Louisa?"

Tiffany shook her head, her blonde hair swishing back and forth. "No. Aimee's not like that. She and Louisa were sisters."

He wasn't sure what being sisters had to do with anything, but he decided to move on rather than dwell on it. He might be able to get a coherent answer out of another employee, not one whose parents he assumed to be smoking some serious mind-numbing weed when they conceived her.

"Was Louisa here the night of her murder?" he asked. It was more than likely but he liked everything to be confirmed.

"Yeah. It's creepy to think about," she replied, her blue eyes wide. "I mean, it could have been any one of us."

"You don't believe Louisa was a target?"

"I don't know. I just think it was some sicko. Louisa was a quiet girl, into her career, you know. She only came here to get a release. It's what most girls do when they don't have a boyfriend and don't want to use their battery operated devices."

"Thank you, Tiffany, for all your help."

She beamed like her answers had solved the case. "Sure, no problem. Did you want me to round up the next person?"

He debated on that. It would probably be easier to have her do it, because she knew the people who worked there. But he decided against it. He wanted to be well away from Tiffany. She drove him to the edge of sanity.

"No, thank you."

A moment later, he found himself alone and moved toward the main event room once more to find himself another willing employee. Just inside, he found Aimee talking to a man old enough to be her father. He snagged her arm.

"Ms. Burnes, what exactly does Tiffany do around here?" The question had been burning in the back of his mind the entire meeting.

Aimee smiled wryly. "She's the events coordinator. I find she has a lot of enthusiasm. She wants to be a wedding planner, ever since she watched the movie. She can quote lines from that verbatim."

He laughed. "I'm surprised your walls aren't painted pink and you don't have pink and silver balloons hovering above you like at end of year formals."

Aimee's laugh, decidedly hoarse from lack of use, filled his ears. "I had to admit, I was a little worried, but she's extremely talented." She glanced around the room. "She did all this. I think she has a real future in the entertainment industry."

He cocked his head and gave her a shrewd glance. "You had no need for an events coordinator, did you?"

"No. But when she dropped by begging for a job, I knew the girl was desperate. I've been there and my heart broke for her. Her body showed signs of starvation and not by desire or need but because she simply couldn't afford food and her school fees. I stuffed her face full of donuts before telling her to come back in the morning."

It was something his wife would have done. One thing was certain, Aimee was a soft-hearted pushover.

***

Sitting at the bar, James tried not to let his frustration show as Jenna Carpenter with her barely concealed body attempted to seduce him. She nibbled on her thumbnail and eyed herself in the mirror behind the bartender. Even after introducing himself, and beginning his questioning, she continued to flirt with him.

No way in hell would he go there. Not that he'd tell her that, not in those words. He wasn't about to offend her.

"How often was Louisa here?"

Jenna took a sip from the glass she'd ordered from the bartender. After a moment of complete silence, she finally answered, to his relief. "Maybe three times a week?" she made it a question, unsure of the answer.

"Is that a lot?"

She giggled and traced a line from the edge of one breast to the other with her finger, trying to draw his attention to her cleavage. "You've never been to a sex club before, have you?"

Praying he wasn't blushing, he shook his head. "No."

"I thought so. You're not very adventurous, are you? You seem like a vanilla kind of guy. I can't work you out. Most men would jump at the chance to fuck me."

He blinked at her unexpected profanity. "I'm not interested."

He fought to hold eye contact with Jenna and not search out Aimee. He'd tracked her around the room for most of the conversation and a few minutes ago she'd disappeared from his sight.

"Well, if you ever change your mind, I'll be happy to do you. I could make your body quiver."

She sounded so normal when she suggested it, as if she'd been bargaining for a used car. The idea made him want to run out of Club X and never return. He wasn't liking the world he was quickly learning about.

Jenna licked her lips slowly, the pink glossy lipstick never moving as she bit down on her bottom lip, oozing sex appeal. He enjoyed the attention she was bestowing on him, but he'd prefer if it came from Aimee instead.

He swallowed hard at the lump in his throat as he tried to keep his thoughts on the job. "Do you know what Louisa did when she came here?"

Jenna shrugged an elegant creamy shoulder and ran her hand through her hair, puffing it up as if it had gone flat while talking to him. "Alone stuff, I guess. I never saw her in any group sessions."

He refrained from asking what happened during group sessions. He had a feeling he didn't really want to know. "Do you know if there was someone in particular Louisa saw while she was here? A favourite, maybe?"

"Sorry, I don't pay attention. If I'm not in a room, I'm busy looking for someone I can take to one."

He shifted uncomfortably. He wasn't used to talking about sex so cavalierly. Never had he once talked dirty to a woman, thinking it would spoil the mood.

There wasn't much more Jenna could tell him and she wasn't offering anything—anything but herself, anyway.

"Thank you for your time, Ms. Carpenter."

She gave him a sultry smile. "Remember what I said, handsome. I could do things to you that you haven't dreamed of."

She turned away and was immediately swallowed up into the crowd. His gaze found Aimee. She was talking to a man with jet black hair who appeared tipsy. The man shook his head adamantly and Aimee pressed a hand against his arm and he jerked away. Their conversation appeared heated. Should he intercede?

He tried to make sense of the scene as he ordered a glass of water from the bartender to quench his dry throat. He was frustrated at not being any closer to learning the identity of Louisa's killer. He was looking for suspects, and perhaps he'd just found one. He took a sip, placing the glass back down on the bar just as Aimee sauntered up, stopping beside him.

He watched her in the mirror of the bar. She didn't look at him, didn't show any sign that she knew he was there as she spoke to the bartender.

"Hey, Jarrod, no more alcohol for Max, okay? Next time he comes over, get him a cab."

The bartender nodded. "Sure thing, Aimee."

Aimee turned and for the first time noticed him.

"Detective Hawke." Her gaze fell to the drink in front of him. "I'm guessing that's not vodka in your glass."

James smiled. "No, water. Trouble?" he asked.

He swore her already flushed face became rosier. "Nothing I can't handle. Max is the club's attorney. He ensures the club's covered legally. Great attorney. Not so great at holding his liquor."

"How are you holding up?"

Shadows haunted her eyes despite her smile. "I just want this nightmare to be over. Did you learn anything new?"

"No. I'm sorry."

She shrugged. "I didn't think you would. My club isn't involved in Louisa's death."

"Can you be so sure about that? You sell a fantasy. People can easily get caught in the web."

Aimee's face turned to stone. He saw hurt in her stormy eyes and regretted his words immediately, feeling the subtle shift inside her that went from friendly to cold in an instant.

"Do you have a problem with my club?"

"I mean no disrespect. I just don't believe in what you're selling. Sex should be something special shared between two people."

She laughed without humour.

"Call me old-fashioned or a romantic fool," he said, "but clearly you've never experienced a connection so deeply intimate with your partner that you were emotionally shattered. The love you share binds you together until you're one person."

"And where is this other half of yours, the one who completes you?" She flung the barb at him, clearly knowing it would hurt.

It had the desired effect. Pain slashed across his heart even as anger and betrayal sprung forward. He should never have opened his mouth. He didn't want to discuss his sex life, or lack thereof. He had only loved one woman and she had let him down.

He turned away, annoyed he'd allowed himself to be baited. She had her views and he had his. It wasn't any of his business if he thought she deserved better than the raw deal she'd been given.

She sat down beside him, close enough he could smell the Jasmine of her perfume and feel the warmth of her body. He tried to ignore her, his body itching to move away, but decided against it. She would probably see it as weakness, something to exploit. He had to remember who and what she was and not allow himself to be carried away with his fantasies. She was the madam of this establishment and he should be mindful of her ulterior motives.

"I believe you are a romantic fool, Detective," she said, her voice soft.

"Haven't you ever been in love?"

Her brittle smile told him more than her words. "How do you think I got here?"

He regarded her pityingly. Knowing her past, he could understand how she could view sex so coolly and detached as if there was no intimacy, only pleasure to be gained.

"I just believe to fully experience sex you first must care deeply for your partner. Otherwise, what you're getting is second best and you're robbing yourself."

Her eyes blazed. "And maybe you're robbing

yourself by denying a natural phenomenon. Sex is healthy. Lethargic. Fun, if your partner knows what they're doing. Surely, a virile man such as yourself can't abstain for long."

"What makes you think I'm not getting laid?"

"Because you're wound so tight." She stood and held out her hand. "Come with me."

"Where?" he asked, eyeing her suspiciously.

"Just come. I promise I won't bite."

Chapter 11

Aimee led him down the hall to a room marked *Private*. The room was painted red, the same as the rest of the club, and a round bed featured prominently. She closed the door behind him and he heard the click of the lock, sealing him inside with her. She touched his shoulder and he almost jumped out of his skin.

Get a grip, he told himself. *You'd think she was crocodile the way you're acting around her.*

Maybe not a crocodile, but another animal with razor sharp teeth. Aimee leaned around his back to press a button on the wall nearby. The curve of her breast pressed against him and he knew he was in deep trouble. The feeling intensified when he heard a buzzing sound.

"Wow, I could surf with you. Relax a little, Detective, and have some fun."

Her admiring gaze swept him up and down with deliberate slowness as if caressing him with her eyes and he fought to control himself.

"I hope the rest of you is just as hard." She

winked, a devious smile on her face. She was enjoying herself at his expense. She stepped back a few paces and he took a deep breath.

What was he still doing here? He should be getting out of there and into freedom. It was what any sane detective would do. But when he tried to move his feet, it was as if they were glued to the floor.

"In today's world, we deal with so much pressure and stress," Aimee said. "I'm sure you hit the gym to deal with your pent-up frustration, but sometimes you just need an outlet. Getting off, as you put it, is such an outlet. It's not just a sexual thing but a state of good health. We all have urges."

She stepped further into the room, facing him and began to slowly undress. Her gaze never left his as she unbuttoned her shirt, revealing the red lacy bra that he'd spent too much time thinking about. Her breasts strained against their enclosure and beneath the lace, her nipples formed small tight beads. The temperature in the room shot up several degrees. His body became clammy as she unzipped her short skirt and let it pool at her ankles. James clenched his hands into fists and breathed in and out slowly. His body rebelled against him, one tendon at a time. His body quivered as if begging him to move closer to Aimee.

She smiled sweetly, seeming to know the battle he was fighting. "This room is called *The Pleasure Maker*, a favourite among most of my clients. It's a room that's just for you."

She backed away from him towards the bed. Sitting on the mattress, she slowly slid back until she was lying in the centre of it, facing him, her eyes flickering with the beginnings of pleasure. He fidgeted uncomfortably.

She pressed another button built into the mattress and James heard the buzzing sound intensify. A small moan escaped her lips as her breathing turned harsh.

"Inside this mattress, there are millions of tiny electrical currents pulsating like the beat of a heart. Harder and harder, they're attuned to locate your erogenous zones giving you a heightened sexual experience…"

She moaned again and her head fell back, her expression one of pure abandon. His mouth went dry and refused to produce any saliva as he watched, unable to look anywhere else as her hips rose with pleasure. His body hardened painfully, all his blood heading south.

Her climax bounced off the walls and rang in his ears, almost following her. It took all his energy to think of something, anything else. She wasn't at all quiet, her mouth open as she voiced her pleasure. Her hips dropped to the bed as she convulsed, tremors taking over her body. She sat up, a sated smile on her face and slowly walked towards him. He could smell her painfully, his nostrils flaring.

Aimee stood in front of him. "…leaving you completely satisfied." She glanced down. "I see I have your attention."

"You have a way of drumming up business. You do this for all your potential clients?"

"Others aren't so obstinate. Why torture yourself, Detective? Embrace your sexual desires.

You may find you like it." She kissed her fingers and touched his lips with it. "Have a nice night."

She closed the door behind her, leaving him alone, waiting for his body to soften. He laughed to himself. He was harder than a rock and so close he knew it was only a matter of moments or thoughts of Aimee before he came.

He took an awkward step towards the door and his satin boxers slid along his aroused flesh as he pitched forward, grabbing hold of the wall in an effort to keep from falling to his knees as convulsions took him over, his whole body shaking with pleasure as he concentrated on not making a sound.

His teeth cut into his lip, and he tasted blood. It seemed like forever before his own tremors subsided and he leaned against the door, feeling sticky. He sucked in a breath and tried to make sense of what just happened. He hadn't exploded like that since he'd been a teenage boy, not yet able to control himself.

Whatever it was, one thing was certain: He had to stay the hell away from Aimee Burnes.

Chapter 12

The highway wasn't busy this time of night. Most of the motorists preferred to use the new freeway that took forty-five minutes off their trip. But for Ben Lake, that wasn't an option. Not only was he a steady drinker but his rig tended to have a few minor defects that he couldn't afford to have fixed. To avoid the coppers or the new-fangled cameras that policed the freeway, he took the longer way to Sydney and on to Brisbane or going south-west to Canberra, whichever was the case.

Lake stubbed out his hand-rolled smoke in the ashtray and gulped cold coffee he'd bought at his last pit stop, which had been a long while ago. His bladder was full from the pint or two he had for lunch, not counting the three or four from this afternoon or the one he had finished inside the cabin of his truck before he started up the engine, determined to make his drop-off in time. His boss had made it crystal clear that if he didn't make it, Lake could kiss his job goodbye.

He gritted his teeth at the knowledge he would

have to make an unscheduled stop since he couldn't find an empty bottle he could piss in. He would need the last of his coffee to make it through the night.

He flicked his indicators on as he slowly moved onto the shoulder, applying the brake. When the rig came to a stop, he jumped out with the enthusiasm of a young man and not an alcoholic forty-something, and stepped onto the dry, coarse grass lining the road. The radio in his truck belted out an AC/DC classic, the warm wind carrying the heavy music into the night.

His headlights allowed him to see no farther than his feet as he emptied his bladder, the feeling so intense it bordered pleasure and pain. He swiped at the swarm of blowflies buzzing around him, then shook himself twice before zipping up, moving away from the ammonia scented grass. There was another foul tasting scent on the air that caused his stomach to roll.

"What the fuck…"

Probably road kill. As he headed back to the truck, nearing the door, he caught sight of a hand lying palm up, darkened by the flies that had landed on the dead skin.

Lake moved closer, unable to believe what he was seeing. A pair of glassy eyes stared up at him, and he knew he would never forget the sight of her. This time, he couldn't stop his stomach from emptying. He was no less a man for doing so. When he was done dry heaving, he grabbed his phone and called the authorities. He wished, for once, that he didn't smell like a brewery.

There goes my job.

Glancing back at the body lying abandoned on the side of the highway, he was sure he'd never sleep again, either.

Chapter 13

James entered the Pig Pen, the nickname of the Detective Unit's workspace, with Darryl beside him. His partner removed the weapon holster from his belt and placed it inside his top drawer. James did the same.

"So, what do we think?" he asked. They'd finished up interviewing the last employee half an hour ago and had left immediately afterward to his immense relief. During the drive over, they'd discussed their interviews and shared their thoughts. Now, all he could think about was finding the nearest shower to complete the clean-up that he'd started in the restroom of the club.

"I think a closer eye on Aimee Burnes and the club wouldn't hurt," Darryl said. "It's too coincidental that her body was found nearby. Someone tied to the club wanted her gone."

Enough to pump her full of Rohypnol, the date rape drug. The tox screen had revealed the truth. With that amount in her system, it was unlikely Louisa had the capacity to fight back. She'd been easy prey for the killer who repeatedly stabbed her, one slice nicking her heart. Her death had not been pleasant or painless.

She hadn't been raped, though the autopsy revealed she'd had sex hours before death. That didn't help, since she'd been leaving a sex club at the time of her murder, though they had a semen sample they could compare to potential suspects when the time came. Doctor Stone, the coroner, had uncovered a drop of blood not belonging to the victim and had sent it off to be tested. Now, they were waiting on the results, which could take days if not weeks depending on the backlog at the lab.

Matt Murphy glanced up from his desk, his brunette hair tousled. Dark circles lined his sharp green eyes. "Heard you're investigating Club X."

Matt was the oldest of the team, in years and experience. James had liked him the moment they'd been introduced. He was the father of two, and one of his daughters had been adopted in the midst of a disturbing case he'd worked. He'd met his wife while investigating the same case, and they'd been inseparable ever since.

James felt a sting of jealously. His last attempt at being happy had been cruelly and irrevocably ripped from him. Aimee's image flashed across his mind before he ruthlessly pushed it aside. He didn't need her clouding his judgement any more than she already had.

Darryl leaned against his desk. "Yeah. It's all we have to go on at the moment, and I've strong feelings the club is exactly where we need to be focused. We need eyes and ears in that club. I say we send Hawke in undercover. What do you think?"

He studied Darryl. "Why me?"

"Are you kidding? Kellie would kill me, Dean would scare the clients, and Nick would enjoy it too much. With you, she'll be too busy exploiting that innocent side to worry about why you're there. You looked as uneasy as a preacher caught with his pants down in a brothel on a Sunday afternoon."

James shuddered at the image. He'd thought he had handled his unease well, but clearly he hadn't. "You think I can do it?"

"I think you'll manage."

"What exactly am I expected to do?"

Matt spoke up. "Whatever it takes."

James swallowed hard. He wasn't sure how to feel about his assignment. Though his heart leapt at the thought of seeing Aimee again, the idea of stepping into Club X as a client had him breaking out in nervous sweat. He'd meant what he'd said to her earlier. Sex was much more than the physical act, at least to him. He wasn't entirely sure he could do it.

Darryl nodded. "I'll do the paperwork tonight." He raised an eyebrow when Matt yawned. "What's with you, Murphy? I thought you cut your hours."

Matt glared at him. "You try being up with a teething baby all night and see how flash you look."

Darryl grinned at him. "Bet Natalie's clocking a few hours with you too, huh?"

"I wouldn't be too snide there, Hill. I believe I saw Mrs. Munroe-Hill this morning sporting herself a rounded tummy, if I'm not mistaken."

His partner's grin faded. "It was a food belly.

She'd just eaten."

Matt shook his head and leaned back in his chair. "I don't know, Hill. It sure didn't look that way to me, and I should know, right?"

Matt grinned at the look on Darryl's face, the blood draining, leaving it pasty white. "I gotta go," he said, heading for the elevator and hitting a button that would no doubt take him to the top floor of the building where Special Crimes and Internal Affairs was located.

Glancing over at the seasoned detective, he refrained from mentioning the little bit of baby spittle on the man's shoulder as he spoke. "Is any of that true?"

Matt made a dismissing motion with his hands. "No, just fucking with him. He's an easy mark. Besides, I don't think Darryl's too far away from joining our ranks. He's just in denial at the moment."

He smiled. He liked all the members of his new team and was thankful they'd been so welcoming toward him—even Amelia, who he'd heard could be as prickly as a porcupine. He only hoped he didn't fuck up and disappoint anyone.

As much as Aimee intrigued him, he had to keep a healthy distance from her. He didn't understand why he was drawn to her. She was beautiful, but so were many others. He wasn't used to such strong-minded woman, preferring the type who needed a bit of protection and leaned on him a little, but Aimee was the complete opposite. Her outer shell was brash which almost had him believing there wasn't anything soft about her. Almost. She was calculating, but he felt her pain as well. She wasn't nearly as tough as she thought she was, and he was utterly taken by her. He sensed her inner vulnerability and knew she would deny she had anything of the sort.

He let out a soft sigh, knowing she had the power to completely destroy his career. James hoped he'd been right with his assessment of her and that she had nothing to do with her sister's murder.

Chapter 14

Kellie peered over the small partition that made up the walls to the cubicles housing Special Crimes and Internal Affairs when her boss, Lewis Carlisle told her she had company.

She smiled when she saw Darryl, tall and handsome, coming her way. It was a good thing she was married to him because one look at him and she wanted to jump into his arms and forget everything else.

He nodded at Lewis, then turned to her. "You got a minute?" he asked, pinning her with his gaze.

"Sure. We're done here, right, Carlisle?"

He replied in the affirmative and headed back to his office, complete with four walls and door. How she envied him some days.

Darryl leaned down and kissed her quickly on the mouth. They had made an agreement that they would remain professional at work, particularly if their cases crossed. So far, that hadn't happened.

She pulled back. "What are you doing here?"

"I've missed my wife. What are you up to?"

"I found the mole who was tipping off Coleani. Luke Jenson. They arrested him this morning."

"That's great, honey."

"No way are they taking back this town."

She felt deep pride, not just because of what she'd accomplished, but also due to the support she received from her husband.

Dick Coleani had been a ruthless dictator who, until recently, had run a large portion of the city. Jenson had not only been feeding information to Coleani but also took bribes and kickbacks from one of his boys, Adam Porter, who was looking to take over his empire. She managed to put a halt on his plans.

"They'll never take back the town, not with you on the case." He studied her intently. "How are you feeling?" The question annoyed her. Yes, anything relating to Coleani hit close to home but that didn't mean she was about to lose it. Just as she was about to blast him for his lack of faith in her, he added, "You've not been sick?"

She blinked at the odd question. "I'm fine."

"Good." He sat on the edge of her desk, his brow furrowing as he studied her intently. "You haven't been throwing up at all?"

"Why, are you? I'm not *that* bad of a cook."

"You're a great cook, honey. I just wanted to make sure you were okay. It's all Matt's fault." He rubbed a hand over his face.

"What's Matt's fault? Did he poison you?"

Darryl chuckled. "No, and I'm not sick either. He just mentioned about babies and I overreacted and wanted to make sure we weren't...that you aren't…"

She held up her hand. "Relax, I'm not, and I'd certainly tell you if I was."

Darryl let out a deep breath. "Sorry, I shouldn't let the thought of us becoming parents shock me so much. It's just I know I'm not ready for that step yet."

"Neither am I, Darryl. Besides, I'm enjoying being your wife at the moment. I'm not ready to give that up to being part wife, part mother. But when it finally does happen, it will be when we're both ready."

"You are right."

"Of course I am. I always am, aren't I?"

"Now you're going too far," Darryl replied, leaning down to give her another quick kiss, which lasted much longer than the previous one and almost set her paperwork on fire.

Darryl straightened, breaking off the kiss before it got out of control. "You about ready to head home?"

She nodded. "Give me twenty."

He started back to the elevator, spinning around when she asked, "If it *were* to happen, would that be so bad?"

Her heart thudded at the look in his eyes. Full of promise and love. She still couldn't believe he'd fallen in love with her. She'd had so many reservations, wondering whether she was enough for him, but Darryl had eased her mind and she'd not regretted it once.

"No. Not at all. I've actually been giving it a lot of thought lately."

She sent him a dubious look. "You have?"

"Sure. Ever since I met you, I've imagined our future. Children with your blue eyes and spirit. It's scary."

"Jeez, thanks," she said dryly.

Crossing the small space dividing them, he took hold of her face, staring hard into her eyes. "That's not what I meant," he assured her. "It's silly, I know, but I'm terrified of something so small and defenceless that's so completely dependent on me for everything. I mean, what if we make a mistake?"

"I don't have all the answers, Darryl. Nobody does. But somehow it'll be all right. When the time is right, you'll make a great dad. I've seen you with Maddie and Seth," she said, referring to Matt's nine-month-old daughter and Darryl's young nephew. "You just have to believe in yourself and hopefully when you hold your child for the first time all your fear will dissolve."

He leaned his forehead against hers and she closed her eyes, loving this form of intimacy almost as she loved their coupling.

"I love you."

"I love you too, Darryl. Whatever happens in our life, know that I will always be by your side. You're not alone anymore. Neither am I. Together, we can handle anything."

***

Darkness enveloped Aimee as she sat alone. She stared at the play of lights on her wall streaming through her window from cars passing by. The air conditioner pumped cooled air throughout her apartment, but it wasn't as cold as her internal temperature.

Louisa was gone.

She hadn't expected to feel so empty, so lost. Louisa had been a part of life since the beginning. No matter where she'd gone or what she did, she knew her sister was out there. Now she wasn't. Aimee was alone.

Despair was a thick, stormy cloud wafting inside her, stretching out its dark fingers to squeeze her heart.

Was this her punishment?

Instead of being struck down, she was to endure knowing she'd been indirectly responsible and made to live the rest of life with that weighing on her heart.

She wasn't sure she could bear it. She'd led her sister down the path to her destruction, regardless of who'd killed her in the end. It had been her own fault. There was no other explanation. Louisa had died because of her.

Even in light of her murder, Ruth appeared uninterested in mending fences. It didn't surprise her. Ruth had never warmed to her. It had bothered her years ago, wondering what she'd done wrong long before she'd begun acting out. Now she saw it as typical, unforgiving and critical. She'd never been able to please her mother and had stopped trying. Why would now be different?

Her club was all she had left.

No one would take it away from her.

What would her life would like without Club X?

The sex industry had been a part of her life since she'd been sixteen and her mother had thrown her out. Young, scared, betrayed, and alone she'd ended up in Sydney where she'd taken a low paying job as a receptionist at a brothel. It hadn't been the upscale establishment she'd made Club X, it had been seedy and foul smelling but also educational. She learned how to close off her heart and use her brain. To allow no man access to what she was thinking or feeling. They could use her body but her mind, heart, and soul were off-limits.

Alone.

The word whispered across her mind.

The harsh reality hit her hard. It didn't make sense. Why Louisa? It should've been her. She'd been the one to lead the less than virtuous life, her name dragged through mud.

Louisa's death hit her harder than expected.

Why had she been there that night? What had she been doing?

Louisa, what have you done?

Chapter 15

Harbour Bay's morgue was located on the ground floor of the LAC building. The chilly room made Darryl uncomfortable. He had never liked being in the room while a body was being autopsied. He shifted his weight as he leaned against the cool, stainless steel autopsy table, which was clean and empty, while Doctor Neil Stone pushed the silver tray holding the body of an eighty-year-old man into the cooler storage.

"What do you have for me, Doc?" he asked.

"Right on time, Hill." The doctor peered at him from beneath his thick rimmed spectacles.

Stone made his way to the small desk tucked into the corner, a large stack of files dominating the inbox. He waited while the man located Louisa's file.

"The funeral home handling Ms. Burnes's arrangements contacted me. Apparently during their preparation of her body they unveiled bruising on her skin, the chemicals highlighting what had originally been hidden beneath the surface," Stone said.

"Bruises?"

"Yes, on her throat and other various places on her body." He pantomimed where the bruises had been discovered on his own body before handing Darryl the file so he could look for himself. "You didn't recall the body."

"No need. I've seen the type before, unfortunately. They were linked to a particular sex act."

Darryl flicked through the photos Stone had handed him. *Damn.*

Fifteen minutes later, Darryl was heading to his car. No way she hadn't known.

Aimee Burnes had better start talking, and he hoped he wouldn't catch her in another lie.

Chapter 16

Aimee glanced up from the stack of taxation papers on her desk to find Detective Hill looming over her. He was a tall man, around six-foot. His face was set in stone, unreadable, like the day he'd come to deliver the news of her sister's death. Her heart plummeted. Did he have more bad news to deliver?

It was late in the evening, the heat of day finally dissipating as the sun set, giving the town a temporary respite. Even now, she had her fan circling above her so fast, just looking at it made her dizzy. To think why the Detective was here sent her into a near panic.

"Detective, what can I do for you?"

"Ms. Burnes, I need to talk to you about Louisa," he said, sitting down in the visitor's chair. He paused as if giving her time to adjust to his line of questioning, or preparing himself for a topic he found uncomfortable. She wasn't sure which she preferred. "The Coroner found something strange on her body."

Aimee's heart pounded.

Does he know?

She'd wondered if it might come up, hoped it wouldn't. She wanted to save her sister some dignity.

"Let me guess, bruising around her neck?"

The detective nodded, surprise crossing his face as if he hadn't expected her to get to the point so quickly. "Exactly."

From the moment she'd heard of Louisa's murder, she'd been waiting for this topic to arise. She'd hoped like hell she could avoid it, not for her sake but for Louisa's. There was something about airing the dirty laundry of a dead person that felt so wrong, and Aimee had wanted to protect her sister as much as she could. She didn't want people to remember her as the Club X victim. Aimee closed her eyes and drew strength from inside her. She would need it.

"Much to my mother's astonishment, Louisa wasn't the poster child for saccharine sweetness. As you already know, she was a regular at my club." She hesitated for a brief moment before soldiering on.

Forgive me, Louisa.

"She liked things rough," Aimee said. "Asphyxiation. Sex games. Whips, domineering. S and M. Things my club couldn't help her with. Not just because of legality reasons but because sex shouldn't need to be dangerous to be enjoyed."

"How did you become aware of her particular appetite?" he asked, suspicion lacing his words. He didn't trust her. She could see that clearly in his brown eyes. She felt the loss of the camaraderie they'd shared in previous conversations. She had no one else to blame. She'd told him she wanted to help, and yet, she'd kept a big part of Louisa's life a secret.

"One night after the club had closed, I heard her with one of my employees."

Detective Hill leaned forward and rested his arms on his strong thighs. "What happened?"

Aimee rubbed her hand over her face, replaying that night in her mind. She'd been tired, her feet dragging as she'd turned off the lights, preparing to lock up. She'd walked past one of the private rooms and heard the unmistakable sound of pleasure. She'd opened the door the find her sister lying on the floor, her legs wrapped around the hips of one of her employees as he screwed her.

The sight had been a shock, but not nearly as shocking as seeing his hands wrapped tightly around her sister's slender neck, squeezing her throat and blocking her airflow.

She'd been outraged that her sister would jeopardise her club—the very thing she had worked so hard for—and that Louisa had been so stupid to do that to herself. Anything could go wrong. People got carried away all the time and before you knew it, someone was dead. She'd been terrified for her sister and had wondered how long she had been taking chances like that.

"I fired him on the spot and told her she couldn't trust that something wouldn't go wrong. She apologised and said she would stop. I never thought to ask her if she was still doing it." Her eyes widened as she took in the implications. "Oh God, has this got something to do with Louisa's death?"

"I don't know. It's just a thought. Do you know of anyone who shared your sister's predilections?"

"None and if I did, they wouldn't be welcome in my club. Louisa knew I didn't condone it. I gave her specific instructions if she ever did that again she wasn't allowed back."

"Do you remember your ex-employee's name?"

It had been over a year, but she didn't have a high turnover in staff and the name returned to her easily. "Marc Trevor."

He nodded. "Thank you, Ms. Burnes. I'll check this out."

"Thank you, Detective. I didn't mean to deliberately withhold it. I only wished to protect my sister, and yet, I realise there's a strong possibility that I failed long ago."

Why had she not followed up with Louisa to ensure she wasn't continuing on that dangerous path? She'd been too self-absorbed with her business and pretending that the incident hadn't happened. Aimee had been the stubborn one when it came to mending fences. What she wouldn't give to turn back the clock. She'd make sure Lou knew she loved her and would've watched out for her sister more. After all, it had been Aimee who'd introduced her into this world with her club. She'd abandoned her sister when she needed her most and that was something she'd never forget. Nor was it something she could ever forgive.

Detective Hill stood. "Are you keeping anything else from me, Ms. Burnes?"

His condemnation hit her full force but she kept her gaze locked on his. "No, Detective. You know all there is to know about my sister. I am sorry," she said. He'd been kind, hadn't labelled her the whore everyone thought she was. Now he treated her with contempt. "I haven't done a lot for Lou in life," Aimee added. "I was hoping to keep her dirty little secret private in death. Whatever you discover, I know it was me who put her on this path. Me alone who was responsible for her death."

Aimee turned away. She was too close to tears, her eyes stinging. She wrapped her arms tightly around her body as she heard him move to the door.

"I know I don't have any right to ask you, but please…when you find the man who did this, let me know," she said, her voice cracking.

"You may lead a horse to water, but you can't make it drink. Your sister made her own choices, Aimee," he replied. "She had a particular appetite that was hard to satisfy. If you hadn't introduced her to this world, she would've found another way, and I can guarantee it wouldn't have been pleasant."

Aimee glanced over her shoulder as he left. Even though he was pissed at her, Detective Hill had been kind. She'd heard his words and the meaning behind them, yet the guilt still consumed her.

Chapter 17

James tried to still the butterflies in his stomach as he approached the podium where Aimee stood. His heart began to race like it always did when she was near. He blushed, remembering how he'd come like a geyser after her private show.

Dressed in another business suit, Aimee's red blouse matched her lipstick and her black knee length skirt fit her like a second skin. The *come fuck me* pumps she wore added to the ensemble. Her dark chestnut hair was pinned up in a chignon, and the pearl studs in her ears added another layer of femininity. His breath caught in his throat when she looked at him, her grey eyes sparkling with predatory interest. She placed a hand on her hip and regarded him.

He was amazed at how she made his body ready just by being there. She didn't seduce him with smiles or sultry looks but he still felt taken. Lust heated his blood until he couldn't see straight. Was this such a good idea? He was hyper aware of her and it took everything in him not to reach out and drag her into his embrace. He imagined his lips touching hers, his tongue delving into her mouth to explore and his dick hardened even more. He wanted her like he'd wanted no other woman before. Aimee had blown him away with her performance on stage and in the solitude of the private room. She was sexy and confident and maybe that was why he couldn't go two seconds without thinking about being buried deep inside her.

He should leave now. Before he did something stupid. He should've been honest with Darryl from the beginning and told him he couldn't think straight around Aimee. But he didn't want to let his new team down, nor did he want a killer to go free. He agreed with Darryl. Whoever had murdered Louisa had done so because of this club. She'd been punished because of something to do with Club X. He only needed to work out who and why.

"Detective Hawke," Aimee said. For all her warmth, it was hard to believe she'd orgasmed in front of him the other night. "Do you have news?" she asked, and he called himself a bastard. It was natural for her to assume he'd come to give her an update. Maybe even announce they'd caught the killer.

"I'm afraid not."

She swallowed hard and glanced away, taking a deep breath before turning back to him. He had to admit she was a master at controlling her emotions. For a moment, he'd thought she might break down.

"Do you have more questions for me or my employees?"

He shook his head. "Not at this time." He shifted

his feet anxiously. Would she believe him? Or would she call him a liar and throw him out of her club? He had one chance to convince her and hoped he didn't blow it. "I was actually hoping to enjoy your services. I mean, not yours personally," he said, and she frowned. He rushed on. "Not that I wouldn't, I just didn't think you were—" He stopped digging the hole and wished like hell for the floor to open up and devour him.

"For sale?" she asked, an amused smile on her face. "No. While everything under this roof comes with a price, I do not."

"I didn't mean to offend you," he mumbled and his cheeks heated. He dropped his gaze to the polished hard wood floors.

The air around him shifted as Aimee moved, her floral scent wafting up to fill his nostrils as she stood before him. His height had him at a disadvantage as she stepped closer and peered up at him.

"I'm not, Detective. I think you're really sweet and kind and it makes me wonder what you're doing here. The other night you were adamant that you couldn't find fulfilment in a place like this."

Her breath tickled his face. She was so close that he could feel her body heat and it would only take a slight shifting of his head for his lips to be firmly planted on her own. "And I still believe that. Doesn't mean I can't enjoy myself. Isn't that what you said?"

"I did."

"Well, you convinced me not to be so close-minded. I'll just ease into things. I'm not really that comfortable but like everything in life, I'm willing to try it once."

As if reading his thoughts, her gaze dropped to his lips and he swore he heard her breath shudder. Her chest rose and fell heavily beneath the silk blouse. Mesmerised, he watched as her tongue darted out to wet her lips. Her eyes softened and they transformed her entire face to something even more breathtaking. James felt a tightness in his chest and he curled his hands into fists in an effort not to reach out and mould that gorgeous body to his until he wiped all other men from her memory.

"Detective," she began, her tone sensual. If she was an inch or two closer, she'd realise just how she affected him. He was painfully hard, his body demanding release, and the longer they stood close together the harder it was to control himself.

"James," he said. "My name is James."

"James."

He stilled, biting off a groan. He hadn't expected to be so turned on hearing his name come from her lips. Now he couldn't help but imagine how it would sound on a moan or a shout.

Shit, he was in way over his head, utterly fucked and not in a good way.

"Are you sure this is something you want to do?" she asked. "Your values are your own. No one—least of all me—should try to change them."

He smiled. "Try everything at least once, right?"

She gave him an uneasy smile. "Right. So, James, what can I do for you today?"

Ten minutes later, he'd joined up, handing his credit card over without concern. Thankfully, he would be able to recoup the membership fee, otherwise the figure Aimee gave him would have made him turn and leave, though she assured him it was well worth it. She handed him a stapled document which was titled, *Welcome to Club X.*

"You can review it later," she said. "It's simply the rules and what your rights are, and those of my employees."

He followed her as she gave him the tour, most of which he'd seen on his previous visit, though it was interesting to see the club during the day. They ended up in the bar she'd performed in. Despite the late afternoon hour, many tables were filled and a slew of naked dancers gyrated on the stage. He'd expected smoke clouds, gaudy red neon lights and shadowy corners. What he was seeing was pale golden light that lit the bar and softly glowed over the tables. The stage glittered like diamonds as did the dancers in a tasteful manner that gave the impression you were there for dinner and show instead of foreplay and sex.

"Shows are on the hour, every hour."

"Will you be performing?" he asked, before he could stop himself.

"No. That's something I only do on special occasions. Although, it's a fabulous workout."

"I can see."

She laughed, the sound sending shivers up his spine. "Are you flirting with me?"

His voice lowered. "I don't know. You tell me."

"I think I underestimated you," she said. "The other night, you were all business. A tough shell to crack. But tonight you're relaxed. Open to possibilities."

"I'm interested," he admitted, and he was. If she permitted him, he'd have her bent over that podium with her skirt around her waist, and he'd bury himself inside her before she could blink.

His erection pressed against the confines of his pants, testing the zipper's limitations. What was it about Aimee that tied him up in knots? He wasn't usually attracted to overtly sexual women, although he enjoyed women who knew what they liked in bed and were equally enthusiastic. Aimee was all wrong for him. If only his dick would pay attention.

"Feel free to mingle. I suppose you can consider Club X a dating service. You'll find many here with the same desires to be fulfilled. Drinks are on the house. Part of your membership. You're welcome to engage or simply sit back and enjoy. There are no judgements here. Be advised anything behind closed doors must be consented to by all parties. I don't have to tell you no means no. Anything you want, I'm happy to arrange, or offer suggestions."

He cleared his throat. "I think I might just look around first. Get comfortable."

"You know where to find me."

***

Aimee tried to push aside the uncertainty creeping inside her. What was this sudden attack of the conscience she was feeling? James was a grown man. He could make his own decisions. So what if she'd pushed him, or rather, seduced him? In the end it was ultimately him who'd requested to join.

Nobody had made him, least of all her.

Still, she couldn't help but feel responsible. He was a nice man. A decent man. Why was she so determined to corrupt everyone she met? She supposed it made her feel better by bringing everyone else down to her level.

He'd acted better than her and she'd wanted to prove to him he was just like every other male. She hadn't felt any better walking away knowing she'd sexually riled him up. In fact, it had made her sick.

He was kind, funny. Sexy as sin. She saw more of his personality now since he'd let down that cop mask he'd worn the night of the mixer. He'd been closed off then, judgemental. Sex was a release, a base need. Not something dirty that made one ashamed.

She'd read him wrong. That rarely happened.

She'd purposely enticed him, wanting him to lose control. He'd presented a challenge to her. Now she regretted her actions. She'd wanted to twist the knife, exert power over him through his body.

She was overly sensitive, yet today, she'd found him amusing. A month ago her life had been perfect or the closest she could get. Now she seemed unsure, out of sorts, questioning not only her decisions but also her feelings.

She should be rejoicing. James was hot. He would reinvigorate the female clientele. Her own libido had been singing.

So, why wasn't she happy?

Chapter 18

Aimee couldn't seem to concentrate on anything but the gorgeous hunk of cop in her bar. She was becoming too familiar with the detectives of Harbour Bay, and there was one she wouldn't mind getting to know better. A single man hadn't held her interest in a long time. Not even the first guy had claimed her attention this thoroughly. It was strange. Usually, she was drawn to bad boys. James was far from that description. She recalled the way he spoke of love, connection, and the intimacies of sex. She'd been jealous. Not just of never experiencing the sensation he spoke of but the woman whom he'd obviously shared such a deep connection with.

But then, she wasn't the type of woman who received promises or even words of undying love. Men saw her a certain way and she'd capitalised on that. Never had she thought she'd ever regret the decisions in her life which had led her on this path.

James made her want something deeper, a connection. But she'd only be entertaining a fantasy if she thought they could be more than detective and victim's sister or client and entrepreneur.

Her feet moved of their own accord until she was standing beside him, her gaze taking in the muscles of his chest and abdomen that his tight shirt highlighted. *Yummy.*

She forced herself to speak. "See anything you like?"

He gave her a long considering look that warmed her from the inside out.

"I might. Take a seat. I could use the company."

"I doubt a man who looks like you would ever be without company."

"Once, you would've been right."

She sat down beside him and had the bartender make her a Sex on the Beach. She loved her vodka beverages. She took a sip.

"What changed?"

"My father died. My priorities shifted. Then I moved here. Haven't had much chance to put down roots."

She studied his face. "Is that something you want to do?"

"What, put down roots? I guess. Never gave it much thought. Why did you come back here?"

"Sydney is a tough market. My product is more in demand here. Plus, I suppose this is the only home I've ever known."

It surprised her to be having such a normal conversation. Nothing sexual or seductive. She'd almost forgotten what it was like.

"Why do you do what you do?"

She twisted her bracelet around her wrist. "It's

the only thing I've ever done. Or been good at."

Corrupting and manipulating people was what Aimee did best. Without those qualities, she was nothing.

"I don't believe that."

"I think that's because you like to wear rose-coloured glasses. Never forget what I am, Detective. What you see is what you get."

He gave her another once over. Her skin flushed as his gaze slowly caressed her body. She knew what he was seeing. Her clothes were provocative but business-like and functional. She exuded sex and capitalised on it, using it to her advantage.

"Do you know what I see?"

She leaned against the bar and smirked. "I can guess."

He frowned. "You'd be wrong. I see a kind woman who hires a bubbly student as an events coordinator simply because she saw someone in need. A woman who feels the need to hide behind her sensual exterior because she's been hurt too many times before, her trust betrayed."

Her spine stiffened. She wasn't sure she liked the way he portrayed her. Not because she didn't like the sound of it but because she might begin to believe it.

"I see more than the body, which is pretty damn fine. I see beyond the clothes. The uniform you wear, while enticing, is a barrier between you and the world, the armour you wear to hide your pain and your heart."

He tucked a loose strand of hair behind her ear. She stilled, having never been touched so tenderly.

A need swirled inside her, longing filling every inch of her. Only it wasn't sexual in natural, it was something more. Something that transcended the physical. She wasn't accustomed to it, whatever it was. Her life was about pleasure, giving it and receiving it. This man was making her want more.

She moved out of reach as emotion swelled inside her.

Her purpose in life was obvious. She would never be more than what she was.

He was her client. That was all he could be. She must remember that.

"I see the grief in your eyes. The unshed tears. Why do you keep it bottled up?"

Her voice was rough. "What good does crying ever do? It doesn't change anything. It won't bring back my sister or make my mother love me. My father will not magically appear. Nor will it erase all the foul words that have been flung at me."

"Words you've begun to believe yourself."

"There is no denying the truth."

James was a man of principle, of honour, unlike her.

Just look at how you got him here. Sex. Yet another reminder that while men flocked to her, indulged in her, in the morning they were gone as if they'd never been there.

He sighed wearily. "You're an obstinate woman."

She smiled. "I guess we're alike in some ways."

"More than you realise."

Chapter 19

Amelia jumped as Superintendent Alec Harris's baritone voice boomed as he made his way into the Pig Pen. "Matthews, I've got a case for you."

Dean raised a golden eyebrow. Amelia's interest piqued. Usually, they didn't get assigned a case in this manner and certainly not by the boss. Alec stopped before Dean's desk, his brown eyes serious and handed her colleague a pale yellow manila file folder.

Dean frowned. "What's the case?"

"Body dump on the King George Highway. I want you to investigate, and take Doyle with you."

Nick immediately stood, grabbing his weapon from his desk drawer and attaching the holster to his belt as he walked over to Dean's desk as his partner opened the file. Amelia joined them, despite not being assigned or invited. They often worked as a team, just as they had on the Butcher case. A photo of a young woman in dry, dead brown grass, covered in maggots, stared up at them.

"Lovely," Nick said.

"How long has she been there?" Dean asked, his attention completely focused on the case. She could see his mind running over scenarios.

"Lividity says roughly seventeen hours, but the lab guys are checking the bugs to narrow down the date. She was found by a trucker who stopped to take a piss. Lucky for us, otherwise, who knows when she would've been found—or *if*."

"Any I.D. found with the body?" Dean asked as he flicked through the different photographs of the crime scene taken from all angles.

Alec shook his head. "For now, she's a Jane Doe."

"Have they already cleaned up the scene?" Nick asked.

"First thing. The damn *Tribute* probably has more photos of the crime scene then we do. They practically beat the first responders to the scene."

The Tribute was the Harbour Bay Tribute, the local newspaper run by Ava Barton, a woman with an axe to grind who didn't care whose balls were in her cross-hairs.

"Great. First Hill's homicide and now this one. I bet the paper's circulation has shot up," Dean said.

Even after years on the job, Amelia was surprised at what people found fascinating. Many times when she was in uniform she'd been called to car accidents and the morbid curiosity of the motorists passing by was sickening. Yet, still, the sight of a car crash or a few mangled bodies didn't slow some people down.

"So long as they don't try to make a connection with the cases and cry serial killer, because that's all we need," Alec muttered.

Dean frowned.

"Is that a possibility, a connection? Does Jane Doe have something to do with Louisa Burnes's murder? A second body? A witness?" she asked, thinking of her own case.

"Who knows? I haven't seen anything to link them yet. For now, let's treat them as separate, which is why I want Matthews and Doyle on point. You, Hill, and Hawke can continue with the Burnes murder," Alec directed.

Dean nodded. "Why are we only hearing about this now, boss?"

Alec's demeanour changed, his body stiffening. His tone was harsh when he spoke. "The body rests on the jurisdiction line. Fallon wanted to take charge. Said we've already had enough murders, as if it was some sort of damn tourist attraction."

Chief Gregory Fallon was Heavenly's own version of Alec Harris. Heavenly was a small neighbouring district of about a hundred and fifty people and the closest town to Harbour Bay. Heavenly Police had such a small budget that they often had to send work their way. Fallon had always been jealous of the boss's standing and the perks of being a superintendent.

Nick's eyes narrowed. "So he thought to keep this one and do what exactly? Heavenly doesn't even have a forensics' lab."

"You know Fallon."

They did. The man was an arse. Amelia wouldn't trust him to investigate a snatch and grab, let alone a murder, considering Fallon still hadn't solved the only murder to ever occur within his own town. Last she heard, Fallon was adamant it was a teenage girl who'd skipped town the same night that he wasn't even looking for suspects anymore.

"I had to throw my weight around to get him to relinquish the body and the evidence they collected."

The last thing any of them wanted was a pissing match. Jane Doe deserved better than the cops fighting over the case. They wanted her to have justice pure and simple. She glanced down at the photos again. She'd been too young.

"Has Stone got the body yet?" Dean asked. Amelia stepped out of his way so he could gather up his weapon holster which he attached to his belt.

"She's on her way," Alec advised. "Give him an hour before you break into his sanctuary. You know how he gets when you start pushing."

"Yeah, he pushes right back and harder," Dean said, smiling. "All right. Nick and I will go to the scene and see if we can recreate the dump."

"Keep me posted."

Nick nodded, then followed Dean into the elevator, passing James on their way who was only just arriving, having spent the morning doing his undercover duties. She cringed. There was a job she didn't want. Just the thought of it made her uncomfortable.

Alec turned toward James. Amelia leaned idly against Dean's desk as the two men shook hands. She still wasn't entirely confident in his abilities. To her, he was still a rookie and couldn't be trusted not to fuck up. He was a decent cop, but he'd come from a small country station much like Heavenly and this was the first murder investigation he'd been a part of. On the other hand, everyone had to start somewhere. What could be better than a sink or swim learning curve?

She also wasn't impressed with learning that Darryl had sent him undercover. She preferred to send Dean, but she understood that James was really their only choice. He was new to town so there was no way he could be recognised by the club's clients. He also wouldn't be made for a cop. James was fresh and didn't have that jaded look in his eyes of seasoned cops—something Dean couldn't hide. But then, for as long as she'd known him, Dean's eyes had always held cynicism in their brown depths.

Darryl couldn't participate for obvious reasons. She wasn't about to explain to Kellie why her husband was spending all his time at a sex club, and Nick, despite his jovial attitude couldn't disguise the lethal predator he was beneath the surface. Nick was a lot of things but he screamed law enforcement.

She'd give James a chance. He'd come with good recommendations and he'd scored high at the Police College so he wasn't a complete novice. He'd know how to handle himself in all sorts of situations and if he could get some fresh leads to investigate, the more chances they had to close the case and get justice for the victim.

"Good to see you again, Hawke. How are you enjoying your first week?" Alec asked.

"It's been interesting."

"The fates must love you. A murder case just when you hit town."

"Or maybe I'm trying to impress you with my amazing detecting skills so I killed the woman and am now going to solve a murder I perpetrated?"

Alec chuckled. "You're quick. You'll fit right in here, son. Anything you need, just knock on my door."

"Unless the blinds are closed, then you run like hell for the exit," she added.

James raised an eyebrow as Alec chuckled again. "As you can see, I like smart arses. If I didn't, it'll be a lonely building."

Darryl exited the restroom down the hall and his gaze caught hers as he approached, silently asking what the hell the boss was doing in the Pig Pen. She gave a slight shake of the head. She'd tell him later.

Alec caught her movement. "Don't worry, Hill, I'm not here to chew you a new one."

"Good. I hear you already ate," Darryl replied.

The older man frowned. "Bloody Marsden. Biggest idiot I've ever met." He ran his hand through his greying hair. "No lick of sense, all brawn no brains."

"Besides that, boss, how're you doing? Bet you're looking forward to that retirement just looming over the hill."

Alec shrugged. "I don't know, some days I think it's all too late. Should've done it years ago."

She frowned. "Come on, boss, don't say that. We needed you here to keep us in line."

"Some more than others, Detective Donovan. I remember giving you a swift kick up the rear a couple of times."

"It was more than a couple, boss. Don't tell me those meant nothing to you?" she teased, placing a hand over her heart and sending him a wounded look.

Alec shook his head and muttered under his breath, "Smartarse."

She was going to miss the old bear of a man when he was gone. Good thing he wasn't planning on leaving town; she'd still be able to get the old team together for beers and BBQs in the summer.

"Everything all right, boss?" Darryl asked.

Her eyes narrowed as she finally caught the slight tension in Alec's body that had remained throughout their joking. She studied him hard and saw the tight lines of displeasure on his face.

He grunted. "Nothing a good convent and an act of God wouldn't fix, Hill."

An eyebrow rose. "Ah, daughter problems again?"

The boss's teenage daughter was as stubborn as her father, as beautiful as her mother, and from what she could gather from snippets of conversations over the years, she and Alec butted heads more often than not.

"I don't think they let you lock up your daughter anymore, boss," Darryl said as he rested his arse against Dean's desk beside her and crossed his arms over his chest. He appeared completely at ease but she knew looks were deceiving. Darryl was more than prepared to leap into action should the occasion call for it.

"They should," Alec said. "Or at least start up a

military school for girls."

"What's Sophie gone and done now?" she asked. She had met the little hell raiser when the girl was thirteen. She didn't listen to any advice given to her, especially her father's advice.

"She's 'hooked up' with some twenty-five-year-old with roaming hands." He caught her shocked expression and hastened to add, "Her words not mine."

"No, that wasn't it at all, boss." Her shock hadn't been due to his vocabulary. "I was just surprised to hear the man still had both his hands."

Alec chuckled. "Oh, believe me, there was a time I almost got out my Glock and shot him where it hurts, but Cait got to me first.

"That's not all, either," he continued. "My darling daughter had her belly button pierced, and you know what went through my mind? Thank God it's not a tattoo. That'll be in a few months when she's eighteen. She's already started packing and doesn't shut up about leaving."

She fought to keep her face straight. The great Alec Harris had been bested by a mere girl. Which was just another reason she practiced safe sex. She was never going to have a back-chatting, stubborn miniature version of herself. She shuddered.

Her heart ached for him. The heartbroken look on his face almost brought her to tears. It must be hard to be a parent, placing so much love and time into a child only for them to turn around and hate you when you try to keep them safe and teach them about life.

Which was just another reason she would never

procreate.

"Give it time, boss, she'll come around. All it takes is a hard dose of reality and they'll come back with their tails between their legs," she said, feeling awkward, because she wasn't normally the sort to offer advice.

"I just hope she doesn't ruin her life while I wait."

"Sometimes that's the best thing," she said. "A person's life is determined by the choices they make, or others choose for them. Sometimes it can go wrong, and on the rare occasion, change the course of someone's life for the better."

Years ago she'd been a tough, smart-talking street kid, who along with Kellie, had been a troublemaker in the neighbourhood. Who knew what her life would've been like if Kellie hadn't been raped and Amelia, determined to catch the rapist, had signed up for the police force. What path would she have gone down? There hadn't been many options.

"Only time will tell, Donovan. If that's your idea of reassuring me, you need to seriously work on that. I could've sworn you were pushing me off the ledge rather than trying to talk me down."

"Sink or swim. That's my credo."

Alec shook his head. "God help the LAC when I retire," he muttered as he made his way back to his office.

Darryl grinned. "You're certainly going to make things interesting around here."

She gave him a great alligator smile, all teeth. "I'm looking forward to it."

"Oh, so are we," he said. "It'll be more entertaining than Saturday night at the movies."

***

Darryl turned his attention to the Burnes case. There was still a lot of work to be done, and no case was simple. There was always investigation, fact finding, cross-referencing, and paperwork, lots of paperwork. And if you didn't stay on top of it, you soon found yourself swamped and about to be swallowed up.

He sank into his chair. He usually had a pretty good handle on things, knew who was lying and who was scared, but what troubled him the most was that he wasn't entirely confident of his ability to read Aimee Burnes. She was manipulative by nature. She had a vested interest in helping them—not only to find the killer if she was innocent, but also to ensure her club wouldn't be tainted by being associated with the murder.

Aimee was an enigma, and kind and compassionate, which was clear because she'd hired Tiffany when the girl had nothing. She could've easily made her an escort but instead refused to compromise the young woman in need. She was also flirty and sassy, intelligent and resourceful. He'd enjoyed his interactions with her. He liked to believe her emotions were genuine, but she was an extraordinary actress.

Could she possibly be lying?

Had he made a big mistake sending James undercover? He'd seen the way the man watched

Aimee, and it was clear he was interested in her. It could work to both his advantage and disadvantage. He only hoped James was professional enough to put his personal feelings aside until the case was over.

It had been over a week since Louisa Burnes had died in that alley and they hadn't found any solid leads, yet. All they had was a hunch that the motive was within the walls of Club X. The search of Louisa's apartment and office yielded no results, and it seemed that Aimee had been telling the truth when she'd said Louisa hadn't shared her life with anyone. Her office was in a similar state, as sterile as an operating room. How could she go through life without so much as making a footprint? Before he had met Kellie, his life hadn't been a party, but he had still *lived*, while Louisa Burnes had merely existed.

A headache pounded and he immediately reached into his desk drawer for the Panadol he kept there for such occasions. Frustration welled inside him. He popped the two white pills into his mouth and washed them down with water from his Charity Fun Run drink bottle, one question repeating itself over and over in his mind.

Who would want to kill Louisa Burnes?

Chapter 20

James sat at the bar at Club X. It had been three days since he'd walked through the doors as an undercover. Three days and still he had nothing to show for it except a raging hard-on that couldn't be sated. Everything appeared above board, yet something inside him screamed that Club X was at the heart of his investigation. He focused on her without turning his attention from the stage. He was careful to keep Aimee in his line of sight at all times, though he dismissed her as a suspect. He couldn't stop from seeking her out, always aware of her movements.

The few times he'd caught her laugh, the sound shot straight to his groin, leaving him in an uncomfortable state and aching for more. She was fair to her employees and understanding of her clients' needs, and he'd witnessed her matching more than one pair who often left the establishment flushed and relaxed. He was surprised and thankful to note she never engaged in whatever went on behind closed doors. Maybe she did when he wasn't there, or when he was otherwise occupied, but he didn't think so. For someone naturally seductive and flirty, her body language was closed off to further invitation.

Even to him, he'd noted with disappointment. Though he understood why. It would do her no good to engage with her clients and from what he'd seen, no one complained. Aimee ran her club with efficiency, ensuring the allure wasn't tainted. People were cut off before they became belligerent and escorted out if they showed signs of being a problem, all without disturbing the other guests. He was surprised at the steady stream of customers no matter the hour. None of them appeared to be murderers. Maybe they were completely off-base? Maybe it was just a coincidence that Louisa had been murdered after visiting the club. But he couldn't shake the feeling he was where he was supposed to be.

He made sure never to come at the same time twice and didn't stay longer than a few hours, making it believable he was simply letting off steam whenever his schedule allowed.

He was still amazed at the transformation it took in the daytime. At night, the ambience was full of mystery and lust, while the daylight hours were sensual and embracing. The mood far from seedy, although that term hardly applied to Club X. It was where fantasies came alive and those who wished to explore could do so without fear of discovery or shame.

A man with raven hair approached the podium, his gait stiff from tension, the lines on his face deep and his expression weary. James stiffened as Aimee touched his arm and his head bowed and shoulders slumped in what James read as resignation. Aimee indicated to Tiffany to take over and led the man into her office and closed the door.

James hated the slither of jealously that ran down his spine. He tried to ignore it but he'd become increasingly possessive over her. He was seriously losing his objective.

Keeping a low profile was almost impossible, harder to obtain information. He spoke briefly with the men at the bar, flirted with the women and stayed away from the employees. He didn't want his questions getting back to Aimee. No one remembered Louisa, which saddened him. The woman only had her mother and sister to mourn her, though it could be worse.

He had no one. Should he die, he had no one to keep his memory alive. He pushed away those grim thoughts. Louisa either spent her time at the club alone, or she met someone here, which meant she had prior arrangements, since they'd found nothing in her phone records or social media to suggest any sort of relationship.

He hadn't believed anyone's social life could be worse off than his at the moment, but he'd been wrong.

After indulging in the dances, which ranged from enticing strips to provocative burlesque with both female and male performers, he'd had lap dances while questioning, without interrogating Aimee's clients, acting simply like a curious newbie without arousing suspicion. At least, he hoped.

His stomach knotted with dread because he'd allowed Aimee to arrange a private room to keep up the guise of sexual exploration, and was beginning to regret the decision. She made him wait in the bar, and he wasn't exactly sure what she needed to organise, but he didn't want to dwell on the possibilities. He assumed she would need to prepare the room for sanitary reasons, and he shuddered, worrying for a moment if he'd be able to pull this off. He wished he could just get whatever she had planned over and done with, the waiting not in the least whetting his appetite. There was only one thing he wanted in this club, the only thing that was off-limits. *Aimee.*

Trepidation filled him at what sweet torture she'd devised, having already proven she knew how to twist a man's balls. He wasn't sure how much longer he could stand pretending to be interested, having spent recent days in a semi-hard state. He was human, after all, but true relief was out of his grasp. He hated lying to her as he chatted with the other women, but never took things further than he needed to. He doubted Aimee would question them, and he was certain she thought him well enamoured, but besides trying to find a killer, he had to ensure he kept his cover. Lips were sure to tighten if they discovered his cop status. To them, he was simply here to enjoy himself, another person lost to the sensual world around him.

He had little desire to indulge in the pleasures Club X had to offer. Despite his hell raising youth, he'd always been a one woman man, though that hadn't ever worked out for him. He'd played the field, slept with countless women and in the end had been left feeling hollow. As his mother had said, he'd woken up. His intentions changed then. To find the one woman who made him forget all others. He'd always had this vision of himself in a strong relationship similar to the one his parents shared. He'd wanted it so bad he'd ignored the telling signs that said something was wrong.

Signs he wasn't encountering now.

He'd encouraged Aimee to sit and talk, and though her words were stilted at first, she had warmed up, entertaining him with humorous stories of her time in Sydney. It felt good to laugh with her, and he realised he'd underestimated her, that she had a lot to offer. Her quick wit hinted at her intelligence. Someone who could run a successful business had to have something more than a pretty face.

Most days he was lucky enough to have her join him for a drink. She was different when they moved from business into personal, no longer maintaining her flirtatious act, relaxing in his company, revealing her vulnerable side. She didn't push him or deliberately entice him, but it didn't stop him from wanting her. He asked about Louisa and their childhood, discovering Aimee suffered from not having a stable parental influence. His heart ached as she spoke of her mother's lack of regard of her, how she'd never had a kind word for her.

James didn't understand. No matter what he'd done, his parents had loved him. He'd disappointed them at times, but they'd always been there for him, ready to pick up the pieces should he need them. He could understand more of how she had transformed into the woman she was now. Not that there was anything wrong with her, but he could see why she needed control, to be the seductress and not the seduced. Why she manipulated those around her. It made him want to cherish her all the more, to show her what a real relationship was like and why he would never be content with empty sex without the emotional entanglements that went with intimacy.

He was surprised when she'd confided in him that she had mixed feelings over her mother's illness. The woman was her only family and despite the past, she was still her mother. He could tell a part of her wanted to reach out but was too afraid of being bitten. He wanted to comfort her but words were cheap and often useless.

He took a sip of his bourbon and Coke, tired of waiting around. When he'd imagined investigating and working undercover, this was not what he'd had in mind. Though there were certain aspects that made the sitting around bearable. Relief filled him as the door to Aimee's office opened and the man exited, his mouth still curved into a frown. He made his way to the bar and sat down beside James and ordered a scotch. He stared down at the phone he'd placed on the bar like he was expecting a call and downed the scotch when it didn't ring.

"Tough day?"

The man's chin jerked up and his lips trembled. "Tough month. My wife refuses to talk to me."

"Sorry to hear that."

The man shrugged. "My own fault. I let the allure of this place get the better of me. Fantasy, my arse. Reality is what matters."

He couldn't help but agree. On the outside, Club X seemed to be the perfect answer to frustration and experiencing life on the wild side, but despite Aimee romanticising her club, there was still darkness beneath. It was why he was here, searching among Aimee's clients to see if there was a killer lurking, looking for his next target.

"I lost sight of that. Now I'm paying for it." The man beside him swallowed another shot of scotch. If he kept the pace he was going he'd be hammered in ten minutes, though James supposed that was the point.

The man looked at him apologetically. "Don't mean to ruin your day," he said. "You're obviously here for a reason and I doubt it's to listen to me cry into my scotch."

"If you hate this place so much, why are you still here?" James asked.

The man stared at nothing in particular, seeing whatever was going through his mind. "Better the devil, you know."

The man had contempt for the club yet remained. Was he waiting for someone? Probably, evidenced by the way he kept glancing at his phone. Not Aimee, he surmised. He really needed to get some perspective. Could such hate manifest to murder? Had Louisa been part of him losing sight, causing him to drink his sorrows away?

"James, we're ready for you now."

Aimee's voice jolted him. He'd forgotten about his appointment. Was it any wonder? He wasn't looking forward to it, but knew he had to make more of an effort to conform. Otherwise, she would become suspicious. He enjoyed the camaraderie he seemed to share with her and knew the moment she learned the truth it would be gone.

Her lips pursed as her gaze ran over his companion. She shook her head and James caught the bartender acknowledge her request to stop serving. His mind flashed back to the night of the mixer and recognised the man as the same one she'd cut off then, too.

Max, he recalled. The stranger required further scrutiny.

Standing, he tossed back the last of his drink.

***

Aimee led him down a hallway and into a room with black paint on the walls. Rose petals covered the bed in the centre of the room. The only other furniture was a large wingback chair in the corner and a Chinese room divider, presumably for undressing or even seduction. The ceiling was covered with hundreds of small white lights, casting the room in a soft glow and providing a romantic feel.

He'd answered her question with a simple request for stress relief but opted to leave the exact details in her expert hands. Now he wasn't sure if that had been the wisest course of action. His heart thumped painfully in his chest. He looked around wearily. He'd half expected to be accosted the moment he entered. He turned back to Aimee, unsure. He'd been that way since the day he'd walked into her life. He hated the feeling. He was usually so confident in any given task, and now he looked to her for guidance.

"Undress and someone will be along shortly," she said.

He unbuttoned his shirt, revealing a flat stomach and trim waist. Never before had he been self-conscious about his body, knowing it was well worth the hours in the gym and the rough routine he went through, but looking up into Aimee's eyes he suddenly worried she wouldn't like him.

You're not going to marry her or sleep with her, so what the hell are you worried for? Once you solve the murder of her sister, you'll never see her again.

Right here and now, he didn't care; only she mattered. He straightened and let her look at him, her gaze caressing his body. His blood rushed south. He struggled not to reveal his thoughts. She flashed him a knowing smile and sent him a wink before departing, leaving him to unzip his pants in private.

He sat on the bed naked, nervousness making him twitch. For what seemed like the thousandth time, he wondered what the hell he doing there. He was an old-fashioned kind of guy. Sex was easy but it was the emotion behind the deed that made it all worthwhile. He loved the connection even long after he left the woman's body. Call him a sissy, but he enjoyed snuggling after the fact just as much as he enjoyed riding his orgasm.

He wanted a relationship like his parents had before his father had died. The way they'd stared at each other warmed his heart and he wanted a woman to look at him like that. He didn't plan on settling for less.

Glancing over at the closed door, his gaze zeroing in on the doorknob, he waited with growing trepidation. What did Aimee plan to inflict upon him? Deep down, he hoped she would come back into the room, but he knew that was just wishful thinking. Although he was slightly relieved that she herself didn't take clients on. He knew she was no virgin, and that was fine by him. He had no interest in virgins but the idea of her servicing hundreds of men left a foul taste in his mouth.

He pictured her in his mind, those grey eyes and her creamy skin. He could see her as she looked the night she had shown him The Pleasure Maker. Her back arched, her high breasts straining against her bra. He could hear the little bursts of breath she made as she neared completion, then the cry that slipped through her lips as she climaxed before him.

His erection saluted the ceiling. He clasped one hand around the base to find some relief. The door opened and he jerked in surprise, suddenly forgetting he was expecting someone. He recognised Jenna and one of the other women he'd interviewed the night of the mixer.

He forced a shy smile as they entered the room, each wearing a satin robe to cover their naked bodies. Two beautiful women. How can a man go wrong? But James knew exactly where it was wrong. He didn't want two women, or three, or an entire harem. He just wanted one—the one he couldn't have.

"Wow. Carrying a concealed weapon?" Jenna

said and the other woman whose name escaped him giggled. If she thought she was being smart, she was well off base. "I like it when a man is ready. It means we get to the fun stuff quicker. Shall we?" Pure lust burned in her eyes. She was going to enjoy this more than he was. She'd been panting after him from the moment he'd interviewed her. "Did you bring you handcuffs, Detective?"

He'd love to be able to send them away, but he knew Aimee would find out and then question him as to what he'd really been doing in her club. The last thing he wanted was for Aimee to know the police suspected someone in her club, or even herself.

He swallowed hard as the two women climbed on the bed beside him. He tensed the moment their hands and mouths touched his torso. Hands moved over his abs and a second later a mouth followed the trail. He closed his eyes against the sensations, enjoying it but feeling guilty at the same time. He imagined it was Aimee beside him, her tongue flicking over his nipple, teasing him mercilessly. Her hands running down his body, dipping between his thighs, cupping him. Someone straddled him, her breasts grazing his chest and his body jolted. The other woman pressed herself against his back, her thighs clamping around his own. He felt kisses being placed on his pecs as the woman slid from his lap to position herself between his legs. His hips arched instinctively as a wet, hot mouth wrapped around his dick.

Her raspy tongue glided over the sensitive underside of his erection until he thought he might pass out. She sucked him and he expanded. She relaxed her throat and swallowed, tightening painfully around him until he was gasping for breath. His hands curled into the satin bedspread as a fingernail scraped lightly over his sac. His hips rose again, forcing her to take him deeper even as the woman behind him tweaked his nipples until they were throbbing. He'd never had a double assault on his senses before and the result scrambled his brains.

His climax surfaced. He was eager for relief, his balls drawn up close to his body, ready to spill his semen. He dangled over the precipice between pleasure and completion and just as he was about to come, the mouth disengaged from his hard anatomy and he heard himself groan in frustration as four sets off hands teased his body mercilessly, bringing him higher and higher.

Again he tried to disengage from the here and now. They could have his body but his mind was all his. He once again brought up the image of Aimee in his head. As he'd done every night since meeting her, he imagined her naked, her nipples pink and beaded, her body wet and aroused. He could smell her even now and thought about what he would do to that creamy skin, how he would kiss and nibble at it like a fine dessert and how as he reached a new height of pleasure he imagined himself plunging deep inside her, feeling her body close around him, the tremors of her inner muscles as they squeezed him painfully. He shouted her name as he came, his body convulsing in a white-hot flash. His body limp and sated as he came crashing back down to earth.

Immediately, he regretted ever getting involved with Aimee and the case. Yes, he had come but that was a direct result to being stimulated. There was no feeling, no emotion, and he was left feeling empty.

Chapter 21

A shadow fell on the document Aimee was reading. She turned to James as he finished tucking in his shirt and she could see the muscles flex beneath the form fitting garment. She'd seen him shirtless, discovered what was beneath that shirt, and if she had her way he'd never wear a shirt again. He was hard in all the right places and she'd never seen abs and pecs so well defined except on the covers of romance novels.

Her blood began to heat and a corresponding wetness between her legs demanded his attention. If just the thought of his torso had her halfway to orgasm, would he even have a chance to slide into her before she went off like a rocket should she ever see him completely naked?

She swallowed hard at the memory of him straining against the zipper of his pants. He was certainly not a small man. She shivered with sensual delight as she imagined him standing between her thighs, poised at her slick entrance.

She stopped herself before she allowed the

fantasy to go too far. He was a client, and the man investigating her sister's murder. The last thought was like a bucket of ice cold water. She could never forget that detail. Lou was dead. She was never going to see her sister again. She blinked away the tears.

"So?" she asked, leaning against the podium.

His gaze locked on hers. "It was better than I expected."

She studied him closely. "Why aren't you satisfied, then?"

He smiled. "Am I really that transparent to you?"

"I'm just good at reading people. After all, that's how I make my money."

He leaned closer to her and she breathed in his scent—a combination of raw male and sweat. She wanted to lick him all over. Her heart beat faster and desire unfurled in her belly. James Hawke was a very dangerous man, at least to her equilibrium. Never had a man affected her as he did and in such a short span of time. A week ago she hadn't known he existed, and yet she felt as if they'd known each other for years. Aimee wasn't usually one for such intense interest. Usually she settled and enjoyed a few rounds of sex before moving on. If the man was good, he lasted a few months until she tired of him.

She had a sudden insane thought. James might be the one to go the distance, the one to stay, and that scared her more than anything. He had a way of disarming her, and she'd like to believe he could be the one to love her forever, but the past was a painful reminder. She couldn't allow the fantasy to take hold. Girls like her didn't get a happily ever after. Her type were always kicked when they were down.

She stepped away, putting much needed space between them. She turned her dangerous thoughts to a much safer topic.

"How is the investigation coming along? I know you can't tell me much but are you any closer?"

He glanced away and when he looked back, she read the answer in his face.

"He's going to get away with it, isn't he? I know there are thousands of cases across the country that remain unsolved. I can't help but feel responsible. If I hadn't opened this club, Louisa would never have been there that night. She would still be alive. This is all my fault."

Strong hands gripped her shoulders. "No, it's not. Did you force her to come here? Did you ask her to walk alone to her car?"

"Of course not," she said. She knew what he was saying but he didn't know what she was thinking, what was in her heart. She had killed her sister.

"Then stop blaming yourself. Blame the person who murdered her."

The heat from his hands burned her skin, warming her body. She stared into his compassionate eyes and her heart broke. How long had it been since someone had cared about her? She ached for him to take her into his arms and just hold her. She hadn't been held in years and she was suddenly desperate for the comfort only he could provide that she could barely breathe.

She stepped away because she hated being needy, and she'd made herself a promise years ago that she would never rely on another person. For twelve years, she'd managed to keep that promise. Now she felt as if her entire life was crumbling around her.

"Are you sure she never mentioned a boyfriend or someone who was showing her too much attention? Someone she felt uncomfortable around?"

She wrapped her arms around her body, feeling more vulnerable then she'd ever had before. "I'm sure. But then, I doubt Lou would've told me if she had. As I'm sure you've learned, we never had a close relationship."

James frowned and she was sure he disapproved of her, which would help her keep him at bay. She couldn't believe she'd ever entertained any illusions about them. Aimee had thought she'd given up dreaming years ago. She was sure she disgusted him. How could she not? Her own mother was horrified over her career choice. She'd learned over the years that men only wanted one thing from her, which her mother had kindly pointed out to her. She gladly gave it to them, but on her terms.

"I noticed at your mother's house there weren't any photos of your father."

Her head cocked to one side, surprised by the line of questioning. What made him bring up her father?

"That's because she burned them all," Aimee said. "My father left us when I was a baby. I'm sure according to every psychologist, that explains all my issues with men."

"Do you have issues with men?"

She gave him a ghost of a smile. "Some would say I like them too much. But I'm certainly not looking for a father figure. Or a mother. I had one once and it didn't work out."

He touched her cheek with his finger and a bolt of electricity ran down her spine. He looked at her with a sad expression and she jerked away. She didn't want his sympathy.

He let his hand drop back to his side. "Is there anything you can think of that could help us?"

Anger bubbled to the surface fast and hot. Her emotions had been ruling her for days now and she was quick to feel anything without provocation. She was on edge and the need to lash out was strong.

"Don't you think I've tried? What do you think I've been doing these past few days?" Anger flared. "Lying on my back like a good whore? That's pretty much all I'm good for."

He caught her arm as she moved to stalk past him. She stiffened at his touch, not wanting or needing him to witness her meltdown. She hadn't meant to remind him of who she was but she'd wanted to sever what little connection they had hard and fast.

"You're putting words in my mouth."

"But not thoughts in your head."

His expression darkened. "You don't know what's in my head."

"I can guess. You're just like all the others. I don't know why I thought you'd be different."

"Those are your hang-ups, not mine."

She struggled against him. "Get your hands off me."

"Aimee, don't go. I'm sorry. I didn't mean to insinuate."

She jerked her arm from his grasp, escaping to her office and slamming the door behind her. She sank to the floor, her shoulders quivering with the need to cry but she refused to allow even one tear to fall.

Damn Louisa for dying.

Damn her father for leaving.

Damn her mother for not loving and supporting her.

And damn James Hawke for making her want things she could never have.

Chapter 22

Amelia pulled her shoulder length raven hair into a ponytail and massaged the back of her neck as she walked towards her desk. She'd been up for the past eighteen hours trying to scrounge up a new avenue to investigate in their quickly cooling case. She had come up with nothing. Disappointment weighed heavily on her shoulders until she was sure they slumped from the burgeoning weight.

She sank down in her chair and glanced around at her teammates. Nick and Dean were both busy with their highway body dump case and she reflected how much work they'd been getting lately. Even though they had busted up a major crime syndicate the hits still kept on coming. Good for the experience, bad for Harbour Bay's tourism and even worse for the victims. She only hoped they didn't have some sort of deranged copycat on their hands.

She looked forward to the coming months when she was finally named Alec Harris's successor. It meant she no longer actively investigated cases but the new experiences should well and truly make up for that. Her entire career had been focused on this one moment when she finally climbed up that last rung of the ladder and became superintendent. Hell, now that she had made it this far without getting her arse kicked to the kerb she might as well try for commissioner.

First things first. She had to get Alec out of here. He'd been meaning to leave for some time now and they all knew he and his wife were looking forward to his retirement. But she also knew he was a career cop and had been doing the job for a long time, so the transition to retiree was going to be a difficult one for him.

She couldn't stop the excitement she felt when she thought about running the LAC. Amelia wasn't naïve enough to think she wasn't going to have to step on some toes. A few of the old timers didn't like the fact that a younger person was about to take lead and the rest of them didn't like that she was a woman. Some of them were smart enough to keep their mouths shut.

The only ones who would back her, one hundred percent, was her team. Over the years that she had worked in the Pig Pen, she had proven herself worthy of their admiration and trust, and they knew she could do the job.

She had earned her diploma in Police Management and spent time in Virginia, USA, at the FBI National Executive Institute working alongside some of the best law enforcers in the world. She'd been worried for some time that the complaint against her made by one of her collars that had brought Internal Affairs down on her would ruin her chance of being promoted to superintendent. But Alec still recommended her.

Amelia kicked off her shoes, her feet hurting, having expanded in the heat. She was surprised to find her entire body ached. She massaged the arch of one foot as she glanced over to where James sat, his gaze glued to his monitor.

"So how's undercover treating you, Hawke?" She'd yet to hear about it. "Did you have any issues infiltrating?"

Nick snickered from the desk beside her, she seared him with a glare.

"Can it, Doyle."

"Yes, boss," he replied.

She liked the sound of that.

Boss. Boss Donovan. Superintendent Amelia Donovan. She pushed away her errant thoughts and focused on James's reply.

"I had no trouble," he said. "Aimee was curious at first but I managed to silence her doubts."

"Good. I don't need to tell you how important it is that we keep an eye on her and the club. The case is growing colder by the hour."

James nodded and fell back into silence. Her eyes narrowed. He appeared to be keeping something from her but she wasn't sure it was work related so she didn't push. She didn't know him well enough to demand he tell her what was going on inside that hard head of his.

She sent Darryl a glance, then shoved her swollen feet back into her flat workmen boots and stalked off into the small kitchenette. She washed out the coffee carafe, then began to grind some beans. She'd just hit the start button when Darryl joined her.

"I know what you're going to say."

She leaned against the counter. "Are you a mind reader now?"

"No. I've just been hanging around you too much, so I actually know you. You're concerned about Hawke."

Amelia didn't bother to acknowledge his comment. "Yes. I'm not sure he's cut out for undercover work. He's new in town, and let's face it, he's not done this type of work before. He's used to traffic accidents and domestic disputes."

"I know and I'm worried too."

She frowned. "Aimee?"

Darryl nodded. "I think he's interested."

"I see. What is your take on her?"

He tugged at his tie to loosen it. "She's hard to read. She's manipulative but I've also seen another side of her. She can be kind-hearted and she's not lied to us, at least not that I can determine. There was one case of omission but…"

She cocked her head to one side. "You like her."

He nodded. "I do. Kellie wasn't much different than her when I first met her. Aimee broadcasts a cool veneer but I'm certain that is not the person she is beneath the surface."

"Do you think she is involved?"

Darryl let out a deep breath. "Hell, I don't know. My gut says no, but there's always the slight chance I'm wrong. In any case, I'm certain Club X is the reason she's dead. Someone there—maybe Aimee, maybe not—had an issue with Louisa and followed her out."

"I think before this matter goes any further we should seriously consider Aimee and finally put it to bed. I don't want Hawke tangling with a potential murderer. If she is involved and she figures out Hawke is investigating her and her club, she could hurt him while he is most vulnerable. Right now Hawke is doing his best to appear like any other client."

Darryl nodded. "I agree."

"Good. You outline the plan to Hawke and get him on board," she said, then gently slapped his upper arm as she walked out.

Chapter 23

Nick looked out across the bar as he nursed his beer. He had offered to buy Dean a drink but after the day they'd had, he had preferred to go straight home. Now alone, Nick reviewed the case he and Dean were working on, pondering how he managed to continue getting up and going to work every day. He'd seen so many horrible things that he didn't know how the human race had survived for so long if this was what people did to each other. He should be in bed, because tomorrow was going to be another long day, but he couldn't sleep. Closing his eyes scared the hell out of him, knowing he'd see the victim staring at him, accusing him for not finding her killer and giving her the justice she deserved. Worse was that he had no one to go home to, no one special who could make all the horrible things inside his head go away. Women hated the reality of what he did and the things he saw.

He'd never found one who stuck around, and it had never bothered until days like this one, when he wished he could curl up inside a woman's loving embrace as he closed his eyes and breathed in her scent.

Shaking his head at his thoughts of being comforted, knowing if Dean knew what he was thinking he'd never hear the end of it. But then again maybe he felt the exact same way.

He never really could tell with Dean. The man was a closed book. With padlocks.

Looking across the bar, past the bottles of expensive liquor he locked onto brown doe eyes of a blonde woman, who smiled as their gaze met. He returned her smile and raised his glass. Shyly, her hand rose and she saluted him with her Raspberry Bacardi Breezer bottle before taking a sip. Five minutes later, Nick drained his glass and stood but instead of walking out the door like he thought he should, he moved around the centre bar towards the woman still sitting alone. She glanced up as he drew near and smiled sweetly at him.

"This seat taken?" he asked and she blinked up at him.

"It's all yours," the blonde replied and shifted her body on the stool so that she would be facing him.

Nick sat down and ordered another beer for him and another Breezer for her. "Nick Doyle," he told her and held out his hand.

A small delicate hand was placed in his as she answered. "Vanessa Wallace."

Chapter 24

Aimee rolled away from the warm male sleeping in her bed. Nausea rose at what she'd done. She'd made a terrible mistake, one she immediately regretted. She'd felt raw after her afternoon with James and had wanted nothing more than to escape to sweet oblivion even for a short while. Now she was back to reality and she felt used, dirty, and ashamed, like the whore she'd often been accused of being. How had her life gotten so complicated? Once, she had taken joy and satisfaction in sex, but now she was hollow. She shouldn't have allowed James to get too close. It was her own fault. She'd allowed herself to care for a man who couldn't possibly love her.

She climbed out of bed, wrapping her favourite emerald green satin robe around her naked body and padded softly out of her bedroom and into the large room that was a combination of her kitchen, dining and living areas. Lost, she had no idea how to find herself again. Now that her life had been touched by James, could she ever be satisfied with her old self, while feeling, wanting something that was out of her grasp?

Sitting down on her teal couch, she stared at the photo on the side table of herself and Louisa when they were younger. A time when her hair had been blonde, just like Louisa's, and they'd looked so alike people had mistaken them for twins. When everything had been okay, or at least near enough—when Louisa had still been alive and she hadn't yet given her virginity away to the first guy that had come along.

She remembered that time. It was true when they said you never forget your first. He had been older than her, and she was so desperate for attention and love that she had mistaken his meagre offering as the real thing. How stupid she had been, how naïve. Looking back on it now, she wondered if she'd ever been that young. After he'd robbed of the most important thing she had to offer, she'd grown up fast, and learned to take what she wanted.

She held the framed photo in her hands. Hot tears rolled down her cheek as she stroked the image of Louisa with her finger. A heart wrenching sob escaped from her lips and she succumbed to the pain welling up inside her. She'd been so good keeping it locked up inside her but now there was nothing she could do to stop them.

After what seemed like an eternity later, she lay sniffling on her couch, hugging the small square cushion and wishing like hell that it would suddenly sprout arms and hug her back—no strings attached. Her throat was dry and sore, her eyes stinging and puffy and her nose ran but she felt better, freer somehow.

She'd made a mess of her life from the very beginning. She'd pushed Louisa away even when her sister had tried so hard to bridge the gap between them. Feeling empty, she stared at the cream coloured wall.

"Come back to bed," a voice said from the doorway of her bedroom and she startled. She hadn't heard him get up.

"You should go home. I'm not good company tonight." She refrained from looking at him. He had been pursuing her for months, and she'd thought at the time he'd only been interested in her because he had some belief that because she owned a sex club her talents must exceed those of her employees. While she was no slouch in the bedroom department, she was sure that wasn't the case.

His rough voice reached her ears. "I'd like to stay."

She was hurting inside, crushed. She had no idea how to overcome the loathing she felt for her life. For once she didn't care about the pleasure of others, only her own, and right now she wanted to be alone with her thoughts and memories—with her grief.

"I'd rather you go."

Daniel McGee moved into the room, his face in the shadows, but the way he stalked towards her with intent sent ice running through her veins and fear congealed in her heart. She stood, not wanting him to have any power over her.

He snarled. "Get in the bedroom, woman. That's what I pay you for."

She spun around to glare at him, the anger she felt sure to be reflected in her eyes. "I'm not your whore. I'm not anyone's whore," she snapped.

And for the first time in her life, she believed her own words. Her mother had called her a whore often enough that she'd begun to believe the worst, but no more. She wasn't garbage. She had worth.

He crossed the length of the room in seconds, his long strides eating up the distance and grabbed her arms, hard. She cried out in pain and almost fell to the floor.

"Let me go," she yelled, struggling against his muscle as he pushed her down onto her dining table, his strong legs shoving her thighs apart as he settled between her legs.

She was weak compared to him. Her training failed her. She was a crafty manipulator, hard edged and cunning. She could give men what they wanted, so long as she wanted to. But take that away and she had nothing, no control, no bargaining chips, just her body, and she was about to be used as some man's pleasure toy.

Her vision wavered, her eyes moist with tears as she bucked wildly beneath him, grabbing at his shoulder length brown hair. Humiliation soured her stomach as her nails scoured his face, digging deep and causing him to bleed, feeling the rough facial hair beneath her fingertips.

He gritted his teeth against the sharp pain, then slapped her across the face as if to stun her into compliance, but all it managed to do was enrage her further.

It was what she needed, anger fuelling her so she

could push him away, holding up her bloody fingernails and shoving them in his face when he made another move to advance. She spoke as calmly as she could, unable to hear her voice over the frantic beat of her heart.

"You may want to be careful about what you do next," she warned. "I have your DNA under my fingernails. You wouldn't last fifteen minutes after I report you."

As if she'd burned him, he backed away, his face contorted with anger and lust, his hands bunched into fists. His chest heaved with the force of his exertion even as he studied her with clear chocolate eyes as if judging how serious she was. When he reached the appropriate distance, she kicked him in the groin and he clutched himself, crying out in pain.

"A little something to remember me by," she said. "Now get out of here, and don't stop running."

He moved as quickly as he could to her bedroom, favouring his testicles. Snatching up his clothes, he left her apartment before he'd even began dressing. She was only vaguely aware of his absence, her body taking a savage shock to the system.

Nausea roiled as she thought of how she'd slept with this man. Tonight had been the first time. She usually avoided anyone remotely connected with her club and she used him to run background checks on potential clients so she wouldn't unwittingly accept a sadistic creep who got his pleasure from hurting women. She didn't allow that in her club.

She would tell her staff that if they saw him, they

should contact security and the cops to have him forcibly removed from the premises. She filed it away with the ordering of new post-it notes and the new line of kinky fashion wear, every thought organised and business-like.

Then she collapsed, her legs no longer able to hold her weight, and for the second time that night she was unable to contain her sobs. She drew her knees up to her chest as the adrenaline slowly left her body, leaving her weak and trembling. Her mind fought to come to terms with what had almost happened.

You'd think I would have learned by now.

Still, after all this time, she was as stupid and blind to men as she'd been at sixteen, always picking the wrong one. Tonight she had wanted company and she'd almost been raped.

She grabbed her purse and dug deep until she found what she was looking for, withdrawing the white rectangular business card. She dialled the number, her heart pounding as she listened to it ring.

"James Hawke."

She let out a relieved breath, finding comfort in his voice. She closed her eyes against the tears, scolding herself for thinking of him, for wishing for a happy ending.

"I'm sorry," she said. "I don't want to disturb you."

"Aimee?"

She sniffled, a part of her finding peace in the fact he had recognised her voice over the phone.

"Are you okay?"

The genuine concern in his voice was almost her undoing as she rubbed her free hand up and down her arm, feeling unclean.

Slut. Whore. The words circled her head. She really needed a shower although no amount of water would truly cleanse her soul, and then a shot of Jack Daniels, her new best friend.

"Do you want me to come over?" he asked. "Meet you somewhere?"

"You'd do that, wouldn't you? If I asked." He was too good for her. She was torn between asking for that olive branch and laughing at how sublimely naïve he was. "Get out while you can, James," she added. "Before this fucking town eats you alive."

Chapter 25

James silenced his alarm clock with a heavy hand to the button. He was surprised he hadn't broken the damn thing. He rubbed a hand over his face, exhausted, having spent most of the night on the phone with Aimee. She'd sounded so distraught—so raw—that he'd felt as if his heart had been torn from his chest. He felt her pain and wished he could soothe her, wished she'd allow him that chance. The thought of holding her in his arms and offering her comfort did something to his insides that he'd rather not examine too closely.

He remembered her words from earlier, her voice filled with pain and her face contorted with self-loathing as she'd called herself a whore. It was clear to him she didn't think too highly of herself, and he was sure he knew where the seed had started and wished Ruth Burnes was a man so that he could send his fist into her face for what she'd done to her daughter. Aimee was a wonderful, caring, beautiful woman who didn't deserve such poisonous words to be thrown at her—especially from someone who was supposed to love and guide her through life.

He knew what it was like for people to have preconceptions of a person, and how hard they were to shake. People would automatically assume since Aimee owned the club that her morals would be as loose as her employees.

He hated that he'd hurt her, even unintentionally. He'd not meant to imply anything of the sort but Aimee had been quick to push him away and planting the idea in her head that he thought her less than honourable. He was sickened that with everything going on that he'd forgotten that Aimee was grieving, and not very well. It was clear to him she'd been oppressing her feelings for days and her tight restraint was slowly unravelling.

His heart swelled at the knowledge that during her time of need, his number was the one she'd called. She may have had other intentions in the beginning, such as warning him away, but it didn't matter to him. Aimee had called him.

Even if he wanted to deny her, to keep from crossing that boundary, he knew she was hurting. She couldn't hide that from him. For the first time since they'd met, she appeared to be showing her true emotions—and he wanted her to know she wasn't alone.

He'd heard the tell-tale sniffles as she battled with herself for control. He'd waited patiently and after a few minutes was rewarded with her voice, much more composed than before.

"I-I'm sorry…about earlier, I mean. At the club. For days, I've been trying to wrap my head around why someone would want my sister dead and I can't think of one damn thing that can help you."

"I understand and I forgive you. I just want to make sure you're okay. Tell me the truth, Aimee, have you cried for Louisa yet? I mean, really cried?"

There was a moment of silence and he wondered if he'd overstepped his bounds. He waited for her to answer, his palms slick with sweat.

"I know she's dead but I feel that if I let go, then she'll really be gone. I know it's stupid."

He closed his eyes at the overwhelming sadness in her voice.

"It's not, Aimee."

"I'm not as cold as you think. I cared about my sister."

"I know," he said. "And I can guarantee you, what I see in you isn't the same as what you probably see in yourself."

He heard her sharp intake of breath. "I think you're a really sweet guy who has blinders on to the world. You stick around me long enough and you'll be tainted too. Just like Louisa was."

"And I think you're a woman who can't see her own worth. You know what a whore is, Aimee? It isn't a woman who can't keep her clothes on, it's one who tells you she loves you while she's screwing another man behind your back."

He hadn't meant to tell her that. The words had just slipped out. He'd hoped to provide her some comfort, instead airing his dirty laundry that probably would have her retreating even further into that cool shell of hers.

"I'm so sorry, James."

He tried to shrug away the pain he'd felt the day he'd learned the truth, but the betrayal was as sharp as ever. He didn't love her anymore. It had died that day, but he hated knowing he'd been played for a fool. It had cut deep and left his confidence shattered.

He'd quickly moved on from the painful memory that had turned out to be the best thing to happen to him because it had been the shove he'd needed to pursue his dreams of being a detective and moving somewhere he wouldn't be judged by his past actions. There was nothing worse than everyone knowing the last thirty something years of history.

As a teenager he'd been reckless, self-indulgent. He'd acted out, drank, stole, and marked the town he'd been born with graffiti, much to the disappointment and annoyance of his father who'd been the chief of police of their small rural station.

Then, at seventeen, his entire life had changed. His father—the man he'd butted heads with more often than not—had been killed by a drunk driver who'd unintentionally swerved as the chief had stepped out of his car to serve a ticket to a resident.

He'd been devastated at the thought that his father had died believing him to be a screw-up. From that moment on, he'd done everything in his power to turn his life around and make his old man proud. He'd graduated top of his class, but all anyone in his town could remember was the trouble he'd caused and how often his father had to bail him out.

No one here knew of his past. He'd been

underage and his father had kept his stupid antics off his official record. He could finally reach out and take what he wanted.

Except, he wanted her. He'd come to Harbour Bay for the advancement of his career but somewhere along the way—meeting Aimee—his goals had shifted. He no longer had the need to punish himself for the mistakes of his past. He knew if his father could see him now, he'd be proud. He no longer had to prove himself. His track record was proof enough.

He ran a hand through his tousled hair as he stood and made his way into his adjoining bathroom of his rental. It had been built in the sixties and hadn't been renovated since. The basin was a lime green and the floor covered with linoleum. He turned on the faucet of the shower and waited for the water to heat.

What was he going to do about her? He'd never met a woman like Aimee. She was smart, beautiful and incredibly sexy. She turned him on like a switch and he couldn't explain his attraction to her. It was more than just lust.

Did he love her?

The thought made James pause. They hadn't known each other for very long, hadn't gone out on a date or even talked in length except for last night, but to him it seemed like she'd been a part of his life for years. Then there was jealously—the green eyed monster. He wasn't a jealous man by nature, even after catching his girlfriend in bed with another man, but the emotion had showed its ugly face the night he'd watched Aimee dance and he didn't like it. Didn't like not having control over his body or emotions. He almost laughed. Who was he kidding? He hadn't had control over anything from the moment he'd met her.

There was no doubt in his mind that she was innocent. He wasn't completely sure why he was so adamant, nor did he have the proof that she'd told the truth in any of their dealings together, but for some reason he just knew. Sure, Aimee was a master manipulator and he was man enough to admit that if she had turned her skills on him, he would probably have no idea she was doing it, but James didn't believe it.

What would her reasoning be? There was nothing she could get from him, had never asked him questions about the case that any relative wouldn't have asked. But James just knew, and the worse thing about that was he had nothing to go on but faith.

Faith in a woman who used and manipulated, a woman who teased and seduced. She wasn't the type of girl he'd take home to Mother, not that he cared since he didn't have a mother to take her home to. But if there was a type good church-going boys were warned to stay away from, it was women like Aimee Burnes. A woman who could turn a man to stone with just one look, just one touch. A woman who was vulnerable and scared but hid it behind wit and control.

She excited him. She challenged him. She was far more than just a madam of a sex club.

What the hell was he going to do? Even if, and it was a big *if,* he loved her, or was falling in love with her, could she feel the same? James had heard what Tiffany had said about Aimee's sexual past, and a beginning like that was a path to emotional dysfunction.

She was turning him into knots, twisting him until he didn't know which way was up. Did he have the same effect on her? Or was she too experienced, too closed off to allow herself to feel anything towards him? He was slowly beginning to see the end of the road and one thing was certain, someone was going to end up hurt. He had a suspicion it was going to be him.

Climbing into the shower, he lathered himself up, his hand lingering over a certain jutting body part. He moaned, the sound echoing in the shower cubicle as he moved his hand faster and tighter. God, he wanted Aimee. More than he should. He could feel his balls draw closer to his body and imagined he was sliding in and out of her. The images in his head were so real he could hear her moaning his name, feel her thighs wrapped around his hips.

James rested his free hand against the cool tiles to keep himself from falling to the floor. He closed his eyes and saw Aimee's head fall back in passion right before her body climaxed, taking him with her. He erupted, spurting into the stream of water. When he was spent, he wearily leaned his head against the cool jade tiles, his heart thumping against his ribcage.

Oh yeah, he was fucked.

Chapter 26

Dean placed the handset of his phone back in its holder and stretched his hands above his head. There was nothing he hated more than being confined to a desk, because he was a man of action, someone who got the job done, and that wasn't accomplished by sitting on one's arse and yabbering on the phone to people without a brain cell in their head. But after the long, stressful, hair pulling, eye poking hours he'd been successful and now he itched to do something—anything—so long as it got him away for the four walls that surrounded him and the desk in front of him.

How did those trapped inside cubicles for eight hours a day manage without turning homicidal or even suicidal before the end of the day? He would go stir-crazy and then just plain crazy.

He stood and his arse twinged in complaint at the sudden motion. Shit, even his bum had melted into the chair. He shook his head, rejoicing in the movement after having become stiff staring at his monitor for the past few hours. He tossed his notepad onto Nick's desk.

"Do me a favour, will you?" he said. "Find out everything you can about a Carolyn Harper. She's our vic."

Nick nodded, looking about as bedraggled as him. He started away, a man on a mission to burn some energy and built-up frustration. He was going to the gym. Maybe he could find one of the smart arses from the tactical team to spar with. He could use the extra ego points he'd get knocking one of them down. When he'd been in the Infantry, he'd always been the first on the ground wherever they were. First to scout the area and first to be shot at if they were seen. He missed those days but he didn't miss the Army with its rigid rules and regulations—rules he didn't play by.

Working his way up, having a stint as an MP, he'd made it into Army Intelligence. He had what it took to go all the way, except for the fact that he didn't play the game as they'd like and wasn't about to put his code of ethics on the line for politics.

That's why he liked being a cop so much, he only had to answer to a few people and the rest be damned, especially if he didn't respect them. He had no qualms whatsoever about telling someone to go fuck themselves if it was necessary.

He didn't regret leaving the Army and every now and then caught up with a couple of the guys from his unit, sharing a pint or two down at Tanner's. It wasn't a fancy five star place like Coleani's had been but it had the best steak you could get for under twenty bucks, and on his salary that was all he could afford.

He changed into his set of grey sweats and a pair of Nike sneakers before taking the floor. He stretched his body, preparing it for the beating it was about to endure. One thing was for sure, he hadn't lost the fitness he'd attained in the army, and he kept himself healthy. He also liked to know he could hold his own in a fight if needed, not that he did in Harbour Bay, but he was a man who came prepared. It wasn't like he had anything better to do either except sit on his couch with a beer and a Victoria's Secret catalogue or some smutty flick from the XXX section of the video store.

He could easily get himself a woman. He was a good-looking guy, nothing flashy like Nick, but he had his own charm. Still, he wasn't looking for anything long-term. While he enjoyed hot, one-night stands, he found the process of acquiring a bedmate tedious. If he thought it could work, he'd write on the bathroom wall, *for a good time call....* It would certainly solve all his sexual problems.

He didn't date. He didn't want to explain to every woman who looked at him with love and marriage in their eyes that they'd better move on. No one would put a gold ring around his finger. All he wanted was sex. It opened up a whole other set of problems, like questions. Every woman tended to see his view on the affair as a challenge, like they could tame the savage beast and live happily ever after. Some days, Dean swore he wasn't speaking English. So, despite Nick's protests, he didn't bother going out anymore.

Often he was asked why he didn't want a permanent relationship. Was it the cop in him who was afraid to leave a loved one behind, or had he been burned by some adulterating slut? But the truth was simple—or at least it was to him. If a man was thinking with his heart or his dick, he wasn't thinking with his head.

He had seen firsthand what loving someone could do to a man, twist him up and make him vulnerable, an easy target. Back in his green days, his best mate had fallen for one of the women in their unit. Not that Dean could blame him, Emma had been the best at everything, loving, kind—hell, he'd been half in love with her himself.

When they'd been shipped overseas, his mate Tony had told him they were going to get married when they returned home, start a family. That was when the trouble began. Their unit had been captured. The art of interrogation stood that females were put on display and tortured in front of the men, inciting their protective feelings, but this case had been worse.

Tony told their captors everything. It hadn't saved Emma, though, not that Dean had expected it to. He'd assessed the situation when they had been brought in and knew it would be an act of God if they escaped. Emma had died a slow and painful death, and the moment her heart had stopped, so had Tony's. Dean witnessed the life go out of his friend's eyes right before he took on their captors, Emma's murderers. He hadn't survived but his actions had enabled Dean and a few of the others from his unit to escape with their lives.

Dean would never allow himself to be put in that corner, would never allow himself to be so vulnerable. Secretly, he thought Murphy and Hill were idiots, lining themselves up for a fall that would eventually come. Wives, loved-ones, were nothing but cement boots as you sunk further down into the dark abyss, struggling for air as your lungs threatened to burst, unable to do a damn thing about it.

It was nothing against Natalie or Kellie. They were both great women, but loving someone was just setting yourself to be hurt. Dean had no desire to feel anything but satisfaction. He didn't want to stay awake at night and ache for a woman, because he couldn't handle it, couldn't open his heart for fear of having it crushed.

As he made his way to the black boxing bag, he pushed aside his fears and reviewed the case. He and Nick had surveyed the crime scene as they'd waited for Doctor Stone to get possession of the body. Fallon's fools had made it difficult and he knew he would be forever chasing down evidence that had been conveniently misplaced or left out of the box they'd signed over to him.

When he and Nick had arrived, they'd found the scene almost picked clean. He wasn't sure if it was Fallon's boys, the clean-up crew or the various animals—including the reporters—that he could attribute that to.

He hadn't been expecting to find much, since the King George Highway was rarely used, and usually only by heavy duty vehicles and locals. Dean was surprised Carolyn Harper had been found at all.

He'd combed the area but Carolyn's murderer was either very good or extremely lucky not to leave any trace. A generic tyre tread was discovered that could be found on over eighty percent of vehicles in Harbour Bay, and they'd been lucky to find that since the car had pulled over to the shoulder but not completely onto the dirt and dried brown grass that had been used to cover Carolyn's body. Whoever this sick bastard was, he hadn't been concerned over anyone stumbling across her.

His hands tightened into fists as he gave the bag a right jab, followed by a left hook and another right swing. The heavy bag rocked back and forth from the power and strength in his hits. The exercise already loosened the knots in his body. Whatever was happening, however bad it got, Dean could always come back here. The bag and everything it represented would always be waiting.

His guts twisted at the bleak future. Finding the son-of-a-bitch who did this wasn't going to be easy, but then, what the fuck was? He didn't get into this line of work because it was easy or fun. But it was rewarding in its own way. He wasn't cut out to be a nine to fiver, to wear a suit and sit at a desk all day where everything was set out from his lunch to his daily dump.

Ending up in the police force had been a natural progression. He wasn't out to make a name for himself, didn't have a hard-on to prove himself like Donovan. Dean knew he was good enough, knew he tried as hard as he could to close a case, and that was enough for him.

He knew he wasn't the best when it came to dealing with emotion. Tears and raw pain brought back too many memories for him, memories he couldn't erase and couldn't heal. He knew his strengths, knew what he could do well and what he couldn't.

Someone out there was missing Carolyn Harper, and his job was to provide answers to their questions. Dean only hoped like hell he could provide them.

Sweat dripped from his forehead and coated his body, his naturally tan skin gleaming in the light as he pounded harder and harder into the hard plastic and the stuffing of the boxing bag. It felt good, freeing him from some unknown oppression.

He hated cases like these. He'd spent so much of his time viewing the world's depravity, seeing what people could do to another human being and frankly he couldn't understand it.

Carolyn Harper was someone's daughter, sister, lover, hell, someone's mother.

He would find the bastard, and he didn't care why he'd killed her, he just wanted justice for the victim. Emma came to mind, and he saw her crumbled on the sandy ground, her dead lover beside her. It didn't matter. Wherever you went in the world, you found the exact same thing, humans killing humans. Some days he wished for his own brand of justice.

"You all right, man?" Nick asked from beside him.

He gave the bag one more hit and raised his arms above his head, breathing heavily, nodding to Nick.

"Immobility gets to me." That was true but it wasn't just desk duty. Watching people you know and worked closely with tortured and murdered, unable to help, was enough to drive any man into motion.

"I found Carolyn's next of kin. She's coming in."

"She didn't know Carolyn was missing?"

Nick shook his head sadly. "No. They had a falling out about a month ago but I did a check and she was reported missing by her roommate. I've got her coming in also."

"Good. It's a start."

"You sure you're all right? You were beating that bag pretty bad," Nick said.

"Yeah, I was just thinking things out." *Remembering things best left forgotten.*

"All right then. Let's go see Doc Stone before the women get here. Hopefully we'll have something to tell them."

"Give me a second to get changed."

Chapter 27

Nick held his head in his hands, thankful for the silence of the morgue. The spacious room, without a single sound, helped him think through the pain of his headache. He was not in the best of moods, and the headache hadn't subsided and was turning into a fully-fledged migraine. Cobwebs continued to cloud his brain.

Just how much had he drank last night? Shit, he couldn't even remember. He still had no idea what happened last night. Why the fuck couldn't he remember anything? Being the detective he was, he'd yanked out his wallet and counted his cash. It wasn't depleted, as it would have been if he'd gone on a bender.

The blonde he'd found, asleep in his bed, was also a huge question mark. He vaguely remembered her from the night before.

The Bacardi drinker, Vanessa.

His brain found her name, lost in a haze.

What the fuck happened last night?

He'd started the evening at Tanner's, the local

cop hangout and the night had gone downhill from there.

He had an urge to bang his already aching head against the wall. He liked his women lucid, not drunk, and he wasn't a one-night stand kind of guy, either. It was a rule of his, one he had made up when he was thirteen and he'd witnessed heartbreak after heartbreak with his sisters, each hurt by a man they thought loved them. He was the youngest of five and the only son. While Donald Doyle loved his daughters, he had wanted a few sons to pass on the family name to, but appreciated Nick the more knowing he'd been lucky to get just one to help balance the scales in his almost entirely female household.

Nick had been raised to treat women like jewels, to step in if a lady needed a helping hand.

Having four older sisters had instilled those qualities in him even more, while hoping there were men out there like him who would gladly help his sisters if they needed it.

Now he had broken a cardinal rule and was feeling like shit. Had he taken advantage of the woman? He was so tanked he was surprised he'd managed to get it up at all. Thankfully, Vanessa didn't seem upset or worried to find herself at his place this morning. Maybe she had orchestrated the whole thing. How many times had he been told never to judge a book by its cover? His sisters constantly told him to be aware, that women these days were aggressive and you just didn't know what type of woman you'd find under her exterior. Nick had hoped as a detective he'd be more observant but like any man he guessed he'd been too distracted by breasts and arses.

Now all he had to do was think how he was going to deal with the situation. He cursed himself. He was surprised he'd been so careless. Shit, had he even worn protection? He didn't recall noticing a condom wrapper lying about.

Fuck.

The last thing he wanted right now was to knock someone up, someone he couldn't remember spending more than a half hour with and didn't even know her last name. The fact that she had come home with him at all wasn't giving her any points in his mind. It was an incredibly stupid thing to do on her part.

He doubted she'd taken a self-defence class. He didn't like to think she was so vulnerable. He made a point to teach the female contingent of the LAC how to take care of themselves, making sure they understood the fundamentals and how best to incapacitate a man. He had done the same for each of his sisters until even Rose, the shy, self-conscious one could flip a man onto his back and crush his balls into mulch.

He would have to talk to Vanessa and get the story about last night straight. Maybe he'd get some answers to the endless questions rolling around his head.

He winced as Doctor Stone slid the metal shelf back into the cooler and closed the door. Even his teeth hurt. He hadn't been aware the doc had completed the autopsy. This thing with Vanessa was really fucking with his head.

Dean stood beside him, lost in his own dark thoughts.

After washing up, Stone turned to them, removing his thick coke-bottle rimmed glasses and using a cloth, proceeded to clean them.

"I haven't been able to determine COD yet. From what I can see, she was a healthy woman before she was taken. Her last few days alive weren't pleasant. I'd say she was held for several weeks before she died," he said, his white brows furrowing. "Her stomach was empty and she was extremely dehydrated. Her lungs showed some recent damage, something I haven't seen before. I'm waiting for the results of the biopsy. I've also sent off a vial of her blood to toxicology."

Nick swore, forgetting momentarily about his own problems. It looked like Harbour Bay had another sicko in town.

Chapter 28

Amelia sat down in her chair. Her table was the furthest away from those, who like her, had decided to enjoy the beautiful warm spring day by sitting under the large white umbrellas used to shade each table on the wharf overlooking the sea-green bay. Further south was the harbour the LAC overlooked, five minutes away by road where the land curved inward slightly.

Amelia pushed her cheap ten dollar sunnies up the bridge of her nose after they'd once again slipped down, too large for her narrow face. She ordered an iced tea and waited for it to be delivered as she glanced at her watch, noting she was a few minutes early.

The waitress placed her iced tea on the aluminium table and offered a smile, one she wouldn't have been flashing if she'd been employed by the restaurant's previous owner, Dick Coleani. A man who'd run several blocks of the town for many years until his death. She smiled as she remembered how it felt to lodge a bullet into his chest. She had no regrets, as the man had caused a lot of pain and heartache.

Looking around the territory that once belonged to Coleani, she was amazed at how much brighter and unsuppressed the area felt. Even though most people wouldn't sense it, she certainly did. While removing him hadn't rid Harbour Bay of all crime, it certainly reduced it. She tore her gaze away from the building where she had taken a bullet. She'd been extremely lucky, but she'd been weak for days even after the transfusion.

In the distance, small boats returned to the marina after a morning of fishing, others only just departing for a day on the water. The heat caused a thin sheen of perspiration to coat her spine.

"Amelia."

She turned as Megan Bailey came towards her, clad in denim, her feet in white sandals matching the *Harbour Bay Seagulls* shirt she wore, the fabric clinging to her body. When she arrived at the table she was almost out of breath. A glance at the large tote bag hanging from Megan's shoulder told her why that was the case. She'd never understood a woman's need to carry everything wherever she went. All Amelia needed was her phone, wallet, and keys and she was ready to go, everything fitting in her pants pockets.

Standing, she hugged Megan. She didn't prefer to hug, but Megan did, so she had learned to endure the strange show of affection. She once again took her seat and Megan sat in the closest one and dumped her bag on the wood plank deck beneath her feet. Her mahogany hair shined in the midday sun, making it more red than usual. Her green eyes sparkled with joy and excitement.

She wasn't entirely sure why she kept Megan a secret, but then she thought of the vultures she worked with and knew she was protecting her, who was undoubtedly a fine slice of meat for them to pick at.

"How are you?" she asked.

"Great. Fantastic, actually. I just came from seeing Riley and I have something for you."

Megan reached into her tote and pulled out a paperback book and handed it to Amelia. The cover showed a sharp knife on a floor with blood on the shining metal.

Murder in the Moonlight by Meredith Baker.

Megan was a bestselling author, and this was her third book. Riley was Riley O'Neill, Megan's editor at the publishing house where Megan's books were printed.

"Hot off the printer. Open it."

She did as Megan asked and found her own name. She refused to become emotional.

To one helluva woman,

my friend Amelia Donovan.

The words were printed in the acknowledgements.

"Megan, you shouldn't have."

She waved her off. "I just wanted to show my appreciation for everything you've done for me. My heroes would still be shooting up the villains like a Western movie, if it wasn't for you."

"I doubt that, but thank you." Amelia found her throat closing and she was glad that they were alone. If she was about to make a fool of herself and cry, at least Megan was the only one there to witness her loss of emotions.

"Don't mention it. Now that's over with, how is everything?"

She shrugged. "About the same. Working that case involving the sex club."

Megan nodded and leaned back in her seat. "I heard about that. She was stabbed, wasn't she?"

If Amelia hadn't known her, she would've thought she was pumping her for information but Megan was only interested because it involved Amelia. All of her books were original and well-written. Never once had she added anything they talked about into her books, and even her main character, Dahlia Blake, was far removed from Amelia. There was no way the two were similar.

"*You* heard that?" Amelia asked, incredulous, because she knew Megan sequestered herself while writing and didn't follow current events.

Megan grinned impishly, making her appear twelve years old instead of twenty-seven. "Stacey told me."

Stacey was her cousin who lived with her and made sure she didn't starve to death when she was writing.

"That explains it," Amelia said.

"That's not all she told me about. Apparently there was another murder, and the girl was dumped by the side of the King George Highway."

"That hasn't officially been ruled a murder yet.

But it's getting there."

Megan nodded. "Wow, Harbour Bay's really going down the toilet. I would've thought after Coleani that maybe we would get some of the innocence back."

"We all wanted that."

"So, heard anything about your promotion yet? Surely they'll be making the announcement soon, right? Aren't you already showing your replacement the ropes?"

Amelia held up her hands. "Whoa. Are you going to give me time to answer any of your questions before you hit me with more?"

Megan smiled. "Sorry. I'm just excited for you, is all."

"When you're on cloud nine, you let everybody know, don't you?"

Megan shrugged. "I just want you to join me up here."

"Yeah, well, it might not be for a while. But it's still on track."

"Bet your getting impatient."

"A little," she said. "I want this so much. But it gives me time to plan—strategize."

"You're not invading Europe, you know." Megan squinted against the bright sun.

"I don't know. You've never been inside a police station before."

"Pissing contest?" Megan's nose scrunched up.

"Exactly. The guys I work with are great. They see me for my abilities and not what's in my pants or under my shirt."

Megan concentrated on her face. "Are you really

worried over them not accepting you?"

Amelia shrugged. "Some of them can be difficult. I see a battle with a few and more than one locker room quip over me, but I'm thick skinned, I'll deal with it."

Her mobile rang, the theme song to Hawaii Five-0 belting out.

Megan grinned as Amelia answered and hung up after a moment. "I've got to go," she said.

"Sure, I'll call you."

"Sorry about this."

"Don't be go. Go keep the city safe, Don," Megan replied, using the nickname she'd given Amelia after their first meeting.

She gave Megan a gentle squeeze on the shoulder before leaving.

Chapter 29

James came towards her and Aimee's heartbeat galloped in her chest. The man completely overrode her senses. Her face heated as she recalled their last conversation. Something had changed inside her. She couldn't name what *exactly* but she knew she was different. Never before had she found pleasure in a simple conversation.

It hadn't started off that way. She'd been a blubbering mess and had probably revealed more than she should have. She'd meant to warn him away from her. She would only ruin his life and instead he'd talked to her, soothed her.

She had no right to accept comfort from him, yet she had, and she enjoyed it. Aimee had never met a man like him before and was positive she never would again.

He was different. She'd been used so many times in her life, betrayed too many times to count, and it had made her distrustful. He was the only man who'd never wanted anything from her, and she wasn't able to make sense of her intense feelings.

She knew James would've been better off never having met her, and she should've never warned him against the city. She should've warned him against her. Aimee needed a warning label tattooed to her forehead, something like, *beware* or *watch your step—danger*.

She offered him a small smile, trying to keep her voice steady when all she wanted to do was cry.

"Detective. Back again so soon? I thought I'd scared you away." It would be better if she had. She hated herself for what she'd done to him, corrupting him for her own needs.

James smiled. "I don't scare easy." He leaned a hip against the podium. "Despite my previous reservations, the place is growing on me. It feels good to blow off steam."

"No word on Louisa's killer?"

His eyes softened. "I'm sorry, Aimee, no."

"It's not your fault."

Aimee's mood darkened even more and her emotions hit rock bottom. She cursed herself. If only she'd never set eyes on the club. She wished she could go back and tell that jerk, her first boyfriend, to fuck off, that she was saving herself for someone who mattered.

Someone like James.

"I wanted to apologise for the other night."

"Don't apologise, Aimee. You were upset. There's nothing wrong with that and I honestly don't mind being a sounding board or even a shoulder to cry on."

She was beginning to believe him, yet a darkness filled her heart. What was she going to do? She was trapped by a problem of her own making.

She cared about him far more than she should.

Aimee allowed herself a moment of reflection. She'd practically rejoiced when she'd first seen him, had considered him putty in her hands to mould, and now she cursed herself at her callousness.

She'd revelled in knowing she could bring men to their knees. Manipulate them. Now it left a foul taste in her mouth and a hollowness in her heart. She no longer had the passion for her work, no longer enjoyed playing the enticing vixen. What once came naturally became a chore she despised.

"So, what will it be this time?" she asked.

***

James surveyed Aimee. She was gorgeous in a cherry red skirt and white blouse. The thick navy belt around her thin waist emphasised her curves. Was it any wonder he was rock hard when he was around her? She was utterly breathtaking and he was a bastard for lying to her.

Guilt ate at him for deceiving her. He wanted no secrets between them, no obstacles. After the realisation he'd come to, he needed to be moving forward. The last thing he wanted was for her to be thinking he was here for mindless sex when all he could think of was her.

"Well, I'm still not sure. I'll leave that in your expert hands." The words almost stuck in his throat and a hollowness filled his chest even as his stomach soured.

For a moment he was sure he'd seen a pained expression cross her face but in the next it was gone and her flirty smile was back. "I know just what you need."

So did he, and she was standing right in front of him. Aimee leaned forward, crossing her arms and leaning them against the desk in front of her.

"Tell me, Detective, why did you move to Harbour Bay? I take it you haven't been here that long?"

"Your sister's case is my first," he said.

"She couldn't be in better hands, I'm sure."

"You flatter me. To tell you the truth, a week ago, all I could think about was the excitement of the job."

"There's nothing wrong with that."

He gave her an appreciative smile. He hadn't been feeling too proud of himself lately, and his eagerness to investigate murders hadn't lasted long when the reality of it hit him hard.

"I wanted more than DUIs and domestics. There's not much action in a small town. Harbour Bay had an opening at just the right time. A significant jump in homicides made it an easy sell."

"Yeah, there goes our tourist dollars. I swear this town has had more murders in the last couple of years than since they first founded the place. On behalf of the concerned citizens of this city, we welcome you."

"I'm glad to be here."

Aimee's gaze flickered about the room as if she wondered why he was here, in her club.

There was something different about her today.

As if her light had been taken from her. There was much more than her sister's death weighing on her and he ached to share her burdens. He wanted to be the man she turned to when life became too much. He wanted to share a life with her.

And he knew that with each new day the space dividing them got a little bigger, filled with lies and guilt. They'd never be together. She would never be able to forgive him for suspecting her club— suspecting her—of having something to do with her sister's murder. There was no way to come back from that and the truth of the matter was disappointing and burned a hole in his chest.

Aimee opened a drawer in her desk, pulled out an eye mask still encased in its plastic wrapper, and handed it to him.

She winked but he sensed it took a lot of effort on her part to maintain a flirty demeanour around him.

"Here you go, handsome. Put this on and someone will be with you shortly."

A short while later, James undressed and sat down on the bed.

His gaze scanned the room. The walls were painted a deep rouge. Several candles had been lit and positioned around the room and he remembered the first day he'd come here posing as a client. Aimee was big on staging the scene and he'd noticed a theme with most of the rooms he'd frequented. They'd all been set up for seduction and romance. It changed his perception of brothels but he doubted they were all as clean as Aimee's and certainly didn't cater to the same clientele.

He breathed in the soft scent of vanilla that surrounding him. This was the part he didn't look forward to. While he admitted to himself he enjoyed the actual act, he found he disliked *performing* on demand.

He'd spent his last few visits in the room off the reception, studying Aimee's employees and clients in secret as he'd been made to endure sultry lap dances before finally going to a private room with a lady of the night when he could no longer keep up surveillance without drawing attention to himself. He felt used. It would've at least made this worthwhile if he'd come away with some tangible piece of evidence or suspicion, but he'd left with what he'd come with—nothing—and James was sure that Amelia was about to have him pulled from the case.

As much as he wanted this to end, a part of him dreaded it, knowing that finally Aimee would know the truth and despise him. No relationship would be able to survive that deception. He wanted to hold off that for as long as possible.

Tying the silk mask around his head, he leaned back against the pillows. A feeling of vulnerability came over him as he lay naked, his vision blinded. He heard the door open and close and the soft padded footsteps as the woman neared him. A shuffle of fabric told him she too was naked, too, the satin robe the ladies wore having been discarded.

He couldn't help his body from responding. The woman kneeled beside him on the bed, one hand steadying herself on his stomach as she leaned over him. Her lips moved teasingly over his chin and down his throat, leaving a trail of moisture from her tongue. James sucked in his breath at the first touch. Something almost akin to pain shot through his body at the contact, his muscles bunching.

The woman took her time, as if learning every muscle in his body, every texture. Her lips moved at the same speed as her hands, excruciatingly slow as they slid enticingly over his skin. It was almost as if she planned to memorise the way his body felt and tasted for future reference. He tried not to go insane. The soft hands glided down his strong, muscled thighs and back up again. The woman leaned forward, her breasts grazing his chest, and his body tingled. James closed his eyes behind the mask to enjoy and savour the sensations.

A warm puff of air floated across his aroused flesh and he instantly knew where her mouth was in conjunction with his body, her hands massaging his taut stomach as he felt the barest touch of her tongue on the tip of his erection.

There was no doubt about it, he was losing his mind. It would've been less tortuous to have just sucked him then and there. Soft silky hair fell across his sex as she moved and his fingers curled into the sheet of the bed.

Chapter 30

Aimee's breath came out ragged, her heart beating a million miles a minute. She didn't think it through, knew only that she had to act. She'd taken something wonderful and in her usual perverse way warped it. She'd never hated herself more than she did right at that moment. She didn't want him to give up on all the wonderful things he'd told her about. He deserved them and more. She bit back a gasp as she caught sight of his gloriously naked body, stretched out on the bed like a delectable sacrifice. He was hard—everywhere. She'd never seen a body so toned and defined. He was a work of art and her palm tingled at the thought of touching him.

There wasn't an ounce of fat on him anywhere. Hard washboard abs lay south of a golden chest coated with a light dusting of reddish blonde hair that surrounded his nipples. She'd seen a hint of that chest before but nothing could've prepared her for the sheer brilliance of it.

Desire built inside her until it pooled between

her legs. Her tongue moistened her suddenly dry lips as she caressed him with her gaze. He was utterly breathtaking—and completely under her control. Nervously, she reached out and stroked a finger down his chest. He felt as good as he looked. Unable to stop herself, she leaned down and pressed a kiss just beneath the left nipple. It puckered and she flicked her nail over the nub. A sharp intake of breath encouraged her and she swept her lips over the broad expanse of his chest to tease the other, giving in to her desire and sucking his hardened bead into her mouth before allowing her teeth to nip the sensitive bud.

He grunted. Breathing heavily, knowing she was about to cross a line neither would be able to take back, she moved lower, seeking out his impressive manhood. Her hands shook for a moment before she managed to get herself under control. She'd done this more times than she could count. Why did she suddenly feel like a blushing virgin? Her stomach fluttered as she breathed in his scent and flicked her tongue over the head of his penis.

He tensed beneath her ministrations as she licked him from base to tip, sweeping her tongue across the drop of pre-cum and savouring his taste. She gripped him tightly with her fist and pumped. He expanded in her hand and he caught her head and held her against him. She lathered him with attention before withdrawing. As much as she wanted to continue feasting on him, she wanted much more of him—every delicious inch of him. Her clit throbbed as she imagined him inside her.

Sliding her body over him, shuddering as she

pressed against his groin. A moan escaped her lips as she rocked against him, savouring the sensation. Her heart beat in her throat as she settled her thighs on either side of him and closed her eyes briefly at the skin to skin contact. She'd never experienced anything so carnal in her life and they'd barely gotten started. Every touch was magnified and she couldn't stop herself from simply touching him, feeling him warm beneath her hand as she stroked his chest, his cheek. Her finger traced the lines of his full lips before she replaced them with her mouth.

She kissed him chastely at first. Her lips skimming over his once, twice—a brief touch then gone. She ran her tongue along the seam. He opened his mouth and allowed her entrance. She slipped inside.

She'd never experienced such a tender kiss. She ached from the sweetness. Tears pricked her eyes. She could shatter at any moment. She might've had sex a hundred different ways but never, not once, had she made love and that's what she felt as if they were doing. It was silly, such a fanciful thought, but it seemed fitting.

Holding the sides of his head, she deepened the kiss. Passion burned hotly. Feeling dizzy, she held onto him as if he was the only thing holding her steady, as if she'd be lost without him. James. Sweet, kind, lovable James. Could she bring him back onto the path she'd deviated him from? She hoped so. He deserved better than her meddling. She'd never forgive herself if she changed him irrevocably. She loved him just the way he was.

She tensed above him. Love?

No, she couldn't love him. She barely knew him, and yet, she was certain she loved him. She also knew this would be their only time together, something she was robbing him of by keeping him blindfolded. Aimee was a sensible woman. She and James had no future. Only the present.

She took a deep breath and sucked in a lungful of air before kissing a path down his throat. Shifting above him, she sat up, feeling empty when her breasts were no longer pressed against his hard pecs. She moved her hips, allowing his length to glide against her swollen lower lips. The pleasure was so intense it was almost painful. She closed her eyes as her body hummed. She could happily stay this way forever, and yet, her body was coiled so tight she might scream if he didn't enter her soon.

Reaching down, she caught his hands, placing them on her thighs. With his hand in hers she moved his palms up the silky soft skin and was thankful for the overpriced moisturiser she bought. She could certainly feel the difference and no doubt so could he. It was well worth the money, though she hadn't thought so at the time.

His hands, directed by hers, moved from her thighs up the curve of her hip and the dip of her waist and over her flat stomach to rest on her breasts, cupping them gently. Aimee licked her lips at the small sizzling sensation she experienced as he took her breasts into his hands. He pinched her nipples and her back arched. He slipped between her folds but didn't penetrate.

James let out a frustrated sound. She felt the

same way. She needed him inside her—now. She was so wet for him that she feared she'd come for him the moment he entered her. Her hand moved to his throbbing shaft and he jerked. She impatiently tore open a condom wrapper and expertly rolled it over it him. She teased him mercilessly, allowing only his rounded tip entrance into the sweetness of her body in hopes of prolonging the pleasurable pain. Once they joined, they were likely to go off like New Year's Eve fireworks.

Strong hands tightened on her breasts almost painfully but only served to excite her more. She gripped his arms as she plunged deep and moaned at the feel of him filling her so exquisitely. Had any man ever felt so good, so right? She was having trouble trying to retain her thoughts but she was pretty sure the answer was no. Nothing about this man was similar to any she'd taken to her bed before. For her, it felt like the first time. Everything felt different, sweeter.

Rotating her hips, he hardened deliciously and expanded inside her. Her head fell back, her long hair falling against James's thighs as she moved leisurely, in and out, up and down. Feeling every delicious inch of him. As if she had all the time in the world she continued her slow excruciating torture. Her muscles clenched around him, trying to hold him there. Her body screamed at her, begging her to ride him hard and fast. But Aimee didn't want to rush. She wanted to experience him—taste him and enjoy him while he was enjoying her. It wasn't about completion, it was about the journey.

And what a journey it was. She'd never

experienced sensations like these. They swamped her. Her body shook with anticipation as she took him into her again and again. Moans escaped both of them, and Aimee could feel the build-up inside her, the tension rising. She rested her hands on his stomach and his muscles bunched beneath her palms.

James surprised her when he sat up, the motion sending him deeper inside her. His beautiful mouth was a scant few inches from hers and his quick breaths were cool against her heated skin. His right hand left her breast to slide down her stomach and lower. His fingers parted her delicate flesh to find her clit and she jerked as his calloused finger made contact. His mouth pressed against the column of her neck and his raspy tongue licked her.

She moaned, unable to think clearly. She was slowly being consumed by passion and pleasure so intense that darkness ebbed at the edge of her vision. She began to lose control, the friction too much for her to handle. James's thumb rotated in a circular motion as she moved on him. Her breath came out in small bursts and she knew she was close.

He moved beneath her, joining her. His hips pistoned up and then it was too much. White stars burst before her eyes and she fell against James. She caught hold of him as her body tightened around his and she violently convulsed. She moved faster, her already sensitive nerve endings never fully subsiding before she was pushing them to greater heights.

James's hips moved with the new pace she'd set,

working with her as she rode him like a prize-winning stallion. Her breasts rubbed against the fine hair on his chest and the contact sent tiny electric thrills through her. Her teeth sunk into his slick, resilient shoulder as her body released for the second time in minutes.

"Holy shit," he whispered, his voice hoarse.

He was still hard within her. She moved faster, her mouth dry and parched. The cords in his neck stuck out and she could see him fighting his own release, as if he wouldn't let go and wanted to bring her to orgasm again. Aimee wasn't sure she would survive it. Her thighs were already shaking from the exertion but she kept up with him.

James grabbed her hips and he moved her the way he wanted, the way he obviously needed—hell, the way *she* needed. She could feel her body tightening again and she moaned in ecstasy.

She studied his face. Even with the blindfold on she could see the fierce expression before her attention fell to the lone trail of perspiration rolling down his cheek from his forehead. Without thinking, Aimee licked up the bead and trail with her tongue, revelling in the salty unique taste and James growled, his hands tightening on her hips as he continued to grow impossibly larger inside of her. She whimpered, his thrusting pushing her high once more.

She kissed him and his tongue rasped against her own before she turned her attention to his cheek. She could feel the slight scratchiness of his short whiskers on her soft skin as she moved her tongue and lips all over his face, savouring him like fine wine as she alternated kissing, licking, and nibbling her way from his face to his ear.

Taking the lobe into her mouth, she sucked. The jerk of James's body beneath hers told her he liked that, so she nibbled her way up and down his ear. Her breasts bounced as the pace quickened and the rhythm changed. She was about to combust, there would be nothing left of her but ash. But at least she'd gone down in a blaze of fire. She had never known sex to be anything like this.

Her inner muscles squeezed hard as James drove her to the brink of insanity. She was wound so tight and every time she moved on him, she quivered. She ran her tongue around the grooves and contours of his ear before plunging the wetness deep into the canal.

He came immediately. She followed, biting down hard on her lip to keep from crying out, but a scream escaped her. It mingled with James's own shout of release. Never before had she experienced something so wonderful, so consuming. Tears burned in her eyes and she squeezed them shut as she attempted to calm her racing heart. Her head dropped to his shoulder as she panted harshly. His arms stole around her waist and brought her flush against him as he held her tight.

She throbbed with the aftermaths of great, unrivalled pleasure and felt spent. She held him, dazed. Slowly, her brain began to function again, the afterglow subsiding as her spirit once again returned to her body and she slowly began to realise what he had screamed during his release.

It had been her name on his lips.

She froze.

He can see me.

But that was impossible.

No one could see through the mask, and his was still wrapped firmly around his head, keeping him in the dark. She began to panic. James must've felt it because he held her tighter as if he meant to soothe her. She'd hadn't meant for this to happen, not like this. She'd wanted James to remember the man he used to be before she'd warped his brain. She realised how stupid that seemed now.

What have I done?

James would never forgive her for this.

It dawned on her that he must've been thinking of her the entire time, believing he'd had sex with a stranger. A riot of emotions broke out inside her and she struggled to capture one.

James. Kind, noble James. She was not the girl for him. He deserved better, much better than a tramp like her. She had to get the hell away from him before she made things worse.

Chapter 31

"Wow, I've never felt like that before," James said. "Not once."

He held her close and tried to make sense of what had just happened. He'd never come so hard in his life and right now he was feeling absolutely depleted. The woman who had sent him to Nirvana remained close and he could smell her sweet body beneath the scent of sex and sweat. Even though he couldn't see her, he felt as if he knew her far more intimately than he had ever known any woman, and guilt began to eat at him.

He didn't want to think about any other woman. He wanted *one* woman. He'd just fucked a complete stranger. He could hear the woman's harsh breathing, her body moving on top of him. They were still joined. It wasn't supposed to be like this. Sex and love were supposed to be special, shared by only two people. A connection he was sure he'd felt, pleasure he'd never experienced before.

He'd been thinking of Aimee. Had he simply projected his desire for her into a connection? No, talent could only account for so much. He couldn't explain it and hated himself. It wasn't fair to him and certainly not to the poor woman Aimee had commissioned for him. He'd gone from believing that to a dick on legs within a week. He had to stop this. He couldn't take it anymore.

The room was silent. Too silent.

If his dick hadn't been surrounded by such heat, and he couldn't feel the delightful weight on top of him, he would've believed he was alone.

He removed the eye mask, discarding it on the mussed bed sheet. His eyes widened and his heart jolted when he saw who he'd just had sex with, who he was still connected to.

He gazed down at Aimee's beautiful body, flushed from their exertions. From her high, round breasts that he had sucked and squeezed to where they were still joined as one, and swallowed deeply.

"Aimee?" he said, as if expecting her to have another answer, another reason for their current situation.

Her startled grey gaze caught his and he held his breath. He could see pain and confusion mixed in with satisfaction. Her breathing was unsteady and she bit down on her bottom lip. A tear rolled down her cheek and he reached up, using his thumb to wipe it away. As if poked with a cattle prod, she jumped up, disengaging their bodies and grabbed a short wrap from the floor before disappearing out the room.

Chapter 32

James chased Aimee down the hall, stumbling slightly as he slipped his pants on one leg at a time. He caught up with her in a few long strides and reached out, his fingers curling around her arm. He catapulted her into the nearest room and followed her in, kicking the door shut with his foot.

He glanced briefly around the room to ensure they were alone, noticing shelves filled with vibrators and dildos, edible panties, and body lotions. It was a sex fiend's wet dream. In one corner sat a cash register and fantasy garments hung from the clothes rack buried in the back of the room. A pink neon light announced *Fantasy Store*, glowing in the low lighting.

Aimee hit the back wall hard as he let go of her. She let out an *oomph* but he had no sympathy for her as he stood and glared at her. She didn't meet his eyes even though he was sure she felt the weight of his stare. She busied herself with tightening the sash of her robe more firmly around her body. A body he'd just enjoyed and wanted a whole lot more of.

Even now, as annoyed as he was, he wanted to reach out and touch her.

"What the hell was that?" he asked. He couldn't hide the anger in his voice.

Unshed tears shined in her eyes as she gazed up at him. "It was nothing."

He advanced on her. "The hell it was."

Her back stiffened. "What do you want me to say?"

A tear slid down her cheek.

He clenched his hands into fists to stop himself from reaching out to comfort her. She'd just deceived him in the worst way and he wanted to know why.

"Why the hell didn't you say something? Why? Is this a fucking game to you?" He lost his battle and gripped her arms, shaking her. More tears leaked out and rolled silently down her flushed cheek.

He was the dumbest man ever. She'd done this to him. She'd tied him up in knots until he couldn't think straight. Did she get some sick pleasure from playing this game with him, or was she merely distracting him from getting too close to her secrets? Had she killed her sister? Not too long ago he wouldn't have believed that but now he wasn't so sure. Aimee had certainly proved she could do a lot of things he hadn't thought possible.

And he'd fallen in love with her. Of all the stupidest things he could've done and he only had himself to blame. And her. She'd seduced him, and the knowledge sickened him. She'd manipulated him, and that didn't sit well with him at all.

Her lips were swollen and he remembered all the times they'd kissed. He hadn't known it was her and he felt robbed. He'd been in her mouth, in her body, and the memory had him semi-hard.

Why this woman? Why him? What the hell was he going to do?

He couldn't come back to Club X again. Their association was over. Any dealings with her or the club could go through Darryl. He was done being her puppet.

Aimee shook her head, her chestnut hair whipping his face as he stood too close. "No. James, please. I never meant to hurt you."

"You think you've hurt me?" he asked, distain dripping from his voice, even though it was true. "As far as I'm concerned, you've proven you're a whore after all."

She paled and he swore at the stricken look on her face. He hardened his heart. He wasn't falling for her lies anymore. He was finally seeing the real her.

"James, don't. If you'd only listen."

"I'm done listening." He dropped his hands, no longer able to stand touching her, and stalked off.

Chapter 33

Darryl turned left and took quick glances at the numbers painted on the kerb as he drove along the street. He found number ninety-seven and pulled his car into the driveway. A man in his early thirties straightened from his position beneath the open hood of his muscle car. His pants displayed grease and oil marks from where he'd wiped his hands. His once white singlet shirt was torn in places and several shades darker. He frowned as Darryl stepped out of his Commodore and met him halfway, wiping the perspiration from his forehead. His skin was brown from working in the sun and his toned muscles bulged. Darryl knew he was looking at someone who worked for a living and didn't spend his spare time in a gym. The man before him had the look of someone in construction.

"I'm Detective Sergeant Darryl Hill. I'm looking for a Marc Trevor," he said, showing his ID with its holographic emblem that shined in the sun.

The man took a swig from the bottle of water sitting in the shade beside his car. "You found him.

What can I do for ya?"

"I'm investigating the murder of Louisa Burnes. You knew her."

He eyed Darryl warily, his posture turning defensive. "I had nothing to do with what happened. That's not my life anymore."

"When was the last time you saw her?"

Marc bent his head under the hood once more. He grabbed hold of a wrench and began tightening a nut. "Over a year ago. Not since her bitch sister fired me."

He obviously had some resentment against Aimee, and it probably chaffed him that she'd kicked his arse out the door.

Bitterness rolled off him in waves. Understandable since Aimee's club had been the last permanent employment he'd obtained, which had made it difficult for Darryl to track him down.

"And you haven't seen her since?"

Marc nodded sharply, and he noticed the muscle in his cheek tick. "That's right."

"Her sister said you and Louisa had sex, that Louisa liked things rough."

He didn't understand the fetish. He and Kellie didn't need toys to get going. Every time with her was like the first time, burning hot, like he would die if he didn't have her. Even now he still can't get enough of her.

Marc shrugged. "There's no crime in that."

"No," he said. "Not until someone ends up dead. Louisa had a particular taste, so maybe she called you to get a number for someone who could help her."

Marc Trevor shook his head and crossed his arms. "Haven't heard from her and there's not many people who would go behind Aimee's back to indulge themselves in some of that action."

"Only you?"

"Yeah, hadn't realised it would be the last thing I'd do at the club. But Louisa was a fine piece of tail. Certainly worth getting my arse kicked to the kerb. Look, if you want the killer, my money is on Aimee."

He raised an eyebrow. "Why do you say that?"

"The night Aimee fired me she was in a real mood. And the way she was with Louisa..." Marc shook his head. "She was flaming mad. That woman has one hell of a temper."

"What happened?"

Marc stared down the street a moment, thinking. "Have you ever had a woman look at you with disdain?"

He shook his head.

"You're lucky. It's not something I'd recommend. I've never seen Aimee lose her temper before but it was spectacular. I remember her lip curled as she told me I was fired. Let me tell you, I almost hit the bitch. I was only doing was doing what *her* sister asked me to do."

"You endangered her sister's life."

"It wasn't her sister Aimee was so damned concerned about. She screamed at Louisa, telling her how stupid she was for doing something so dangerous, and that she needed help. She told her if Louisa ever did anything like that in her club again she would no longer be welcome there. The last thing I heard was Aimee telling Louisa that she could've destroyed her club." His gaze held Darryl's and he said, "Always her fucking club."

He made a mental note. Was Aimee so protective of her club that she'd do anything to protect it? Had she caught her sister and decided to stop Louisa once and for all? He didn't like how this new information cast Aimee in a less than favourable light, but he was a detective and he couldn't afford to allow himself to have feelings about the matter one way or the other. His only job was to follow the evidence and get justice for his victim.

He liked Aimee. But if she had anything to do with her sister's death, he would nail her arse to the wall as he would any other guilty party.

"Would you be willing to provide a DNA sample to corroborate your story?"

Trevor gave him a hard stare before picking up a grease rag from the hood of the car and wiping his forehead. He handed the rag to Darryl.

"There. Anything else?"

He shook his head. "Thank you, Mr. Trevor. If I have further questions, you'll be hearing from me."

He grunted then continued working on his car while Darryl left.

Chapter 34

Aimee washed her face in the small basin of the private bathroom attached to her office. The moment she dried her skin, she continued to weep. She couldn't stop crying, her eyes red and irritated. She hugged her body as she stared at her reflection, not liking what she saw, the person she'd become. She'd hurt the one man she would ever care about and he refused to let her explain.

Pain slashed through her. She deserved everything that was coming to her.

"Aimee," Tiffany called out, and Aimee exited her office in time to see Darryl Hill walking towards her, his expression foreboding.

Aimee was sure she heard Tiffany whimper beside her. She could understand the younger woman's reaction. His gaze pinned her, not allowing her to run, not that she'd dare—especially when he looked like that. He'd chase her down before she got more than a few feet away.

Aimee swallowed, her mouth dry and her palms damp. What had she done to receive the wrath of

Detective Hill? An uneasy thought slithered down her spine. Did he know about her relationship with James? Was he angry at her for sleeping with his partner? She hadn't considered that her actions might get James in trouble. There must be some sort of rule that forbade romantic entanglements between a cop and a person linked to one of their cases.

Her heart pounded in her chest as her mind raced. Without breaking stride, his large hand gripped her upper arm—much as James had— squeezing gently but pinching her flesh as he directed her into her office.

She went along willingly, even as her body plunged into survival mode.

Panic welled inside her.

***

When Aimee stumbled into him, Darryl's hand slipped, and he realised it was the first time in a year he'd copped a feel on a woman who wasn't his wife. Her top covered her cleavage but he knew she possessed a decent cup size that her sunflower yellow blouse kept hidden.

He released her like she had burned him and she took a few steps back, rubbing her arm. She straightened her spine, ready to take any situation on, but he could see the uncertainty, as if she didn't quite know what to make of him or the situation.

He liked that, having caught her off guard. Darryl found she showed a whole other side of herself when she didn't have the time to mask her personality. He glared at her, making her uncomfortable. He was angry at her for lying, mad at her for being involved in the case, even if she didn't have a choice, mad at her for being less than squeaky clean.

Darryl had wanted her to be innocent for the sake of Detective Hawke. He knew James had an infatuation with Aimee and didn't want to see the man get hurt. Not that he could see their relationship ending happily, but then, he hadn't thought he'd had a future with Kellie, either, and now look where he was.

Indecision coated his insides and left him feeling useless and on edge. After all they had discovered about Louisa and Aimee Burnes, he still couldn't make up his mind about whether or not she was innocent. Every time he came to her with evidence, she had an easy answer and he was unsure whether or not to trust her. She seemed to him so earnest but his pessimistic side said she could very well have her own agenda. He only hoped James knew what he was doing.

"Is this about James?" she asked.

"What about him?"

A blush rose from the collar of her shirt. "I just thought…nothing."

Oh shit. They'd had sex.

There was no doubt in his mind that Aimee and James had just entered into something complicated. He let out a deep breath and rubbed his eyes. He had an overwhelming desire to smack James over the back of his head for being so stupid. Although, she appeared genuinely concerned, and he wondered how she felt about him. But how did he feel about her? It was clear he desired her but did he want something more, something deeper? Did she? He was sure one of them would walk away with a broken heart.

"I spoke with Trevor," he said. "It appears you forgot to mention certain aspects of that night to me."

Aimee frowned. "I told you everything."

"How about the fact that you were extremely pissed at your sister for endangering your club? According to Trevor, you were mad enough to kill that night." Darryl stepped closer, trying to intimidate her.

Aimee stepped away and crossed her arms under her breasts, rubbing her palms up and down her arms as if suddenly cold. Since the temperature outside was humid, and the inside of the club not much cooler, Darryl knew she was simply uncomfortable.

"I didn't lie to you, Detective," Aimee said. "I omitted unintentionally. Again. I only told you what I thought was important to the case. I admit I lashed out and may have said some things in anger, but I honestly don't remember them."

This was the second time he'd caught her in a lie—or in her words, an omission. So, why was he not taking her back to the LAC for an in-depth interview to uncover the rest of her lies like he would anyone else? Because she *wasn't* anyone else. Dammit. James wasn't the only one too involved in the case.

"What lengths would you go to protect your

club, Ms. Burnes?" Darryl asked.

She sat down in the chair behind her desk warily, as if she'd aged in the past few minutes. "It depends on the threat. When Coleani was in power, I paid him twelve thousand a month for his protection because I felt the price too high not to. I knew the type of man he was and what could happen if I didn't. I had a duty to my employees, not only to keep them employed but safe also. So I bowed to his wishes."

That surprised him. He'd not considered that Aimee's business might've been on Coleani's list of shake-downs. The warehouse wasn't in the neighbourhood he'd reigned over, but then she would've been in direct competition with his own business, the Satin Thong—a low-rent strip club.

"Isn't it true that Louisa could've cost you your permits, your insurance? You could've lost everything."

"Yes. Did you expect me to lie?"

"You've done so before."

"Not with intention. Yes, the legalities of what she'd engaged in are staggering. In my business, reputation is everything. One hint of impropriety and Club X will suffer. I would be denied licences and without those my employees cannot work legally. But Louisa had no idea she was risking all that."

"Didn't she? Isn't it possible she'd done so to purposely to play your hand? You and Louisa were never close. She could've been harbouring deep resentment towards you."

He posed the questions and studied her face

closely for a reaction. Her jaw tightened but otherwise she showed no outward feeling to his accusations.

"Louisa didn't have a mean bone in her body. Certainly wasn't vengeful to whatever slight she may have perceived against me. She was cool and controlled. I screamed at her that night, over a year ago. I was scared of what I'd seen. It was dangerous, to her and the club."

"Yet, you chose to ignore her deadly pursuits. Instead of providing her a safe environment as you've done for complete strangers, you were concerned over legalities and reputation."

Aimee's face paled as she stared at him. "I know you don't like me, Detective Hill, and you probably think I've gotten my claws into James, but I'm not nearly as awful and conniving as you make me sound. I love my club, but I loved my sister more. I'd sell it tomorrow if that meant getting Lou back."

"I don't have an opinion on you one way or the other," he said, feeling like crap that he'd hurt her. "You're a person of interest in this case and I can't afford to let my judgement be clouded."

"As if it isn't already. All you people are the same with your preconceptions. I know what people think when they look at me. Some have even said them to my face. Slut. Whore. Worthless."

She stopped and swallowed hard. He knew where she'd heard some of those words—from her own mother. Ruth Burnes didn't seem like the forgiving type. The barbs hurt, cut deep. Even now, he could see she half believed them.

"I've done things I'm not proud of but I have a

clean conscience which is more than I can say about some," she added.

The fire died from her eyes. She wasn't the same woman he'd met weeks ago. Gone was the overly sexual, sultry dancing madam and in her place a subdued version who seemed to be looking back on her life and counting every mistake she'd ever made.

Was that James's influence, or just the aftermath of her sister's untimely death?

He inclined his head towards her. "Trevor said he'd not seen your sister since that night and none of your employees admitted to having Louisa as a client. Is it possible she may have been sleeping with one of your clients?"

Aimee blinked at the sudden change of conversation. "It is entirely possible. I charge a membership fee, depending on the client and their specific requirements. What they do here is up to them. They can choose to be alone, in a group, or merely an observer."

Darryl shuddered, and Aimee smiled at his discomfort.

"This is a house of debauchery," she said. "The possibilities are endless. Sexual gratification comes in all forms. It might not be your cup of tea, Detective, but I can guarantee it is someone else's."

"How closely do you look into the pasts of your clients?"

"I have all my clients checked out thoroughly before membership is offered. Anyone who has a history of violence is out, but other than that, if they can pay..." Aimee shrugged and glanced away.

She was obviously feeling guilty that she would take money from just about anyone.

"How do you do the background check?"

Aimee leaned back, her dark hair pulled away from her face with a high clip, her ponytail hanging down her back. "I used to have a private investigator."

Darryl raised an eyebrow. "Used to?"

"It didn't work out."

Darryl could tell there was more, but he didn't push.

"We'll need a list of your clients," he said.

"You know I can't do that for many reasons. The least of which is my club," she added, then stared at him hard, with uncompromising eyes. "I'd hand that information over to you freely if it wasn't a lawsuit waiting to happen. People here expect anonymity and would prefer it to remain that way. You'll need a subpoena. But I'll have the list ready when you come back."

Darryl nodded. "Thank you."

Aimee sent him a stare made from pure steel. "We weren't particularly close, Detective, but as they say…blood is thicker than water, and contrary to your belief, I didn't spill hers."

Chapter 35

James slammed his desk drawer shut, the sound reverberating throughout the empty office. He didn't feel any better, his body brittle and tense. What game was she playing? Anger consumed him, radiating from him in waves. He'd messed up and he knew it. Worse yet, it wasn't just with his case but in his personal life as well.

Listen? She wanted him to listen. To what, her excuses? He was done with her.

So why the hell was his heart aching? He rubbed at his chest.

Darryl stalked across the room and headed straight for him, then placed his palms flat on the desk, leaning in. His anger washed over James, slamming against him like gale force winds.

"You better know what you're doing," he said.

James didn't need to ask what he meant. It was obvious in the disapproving look he was casting his way.

"I made a mistake," he said. He didn't want to talk about Aimee. He was raw and bruised. She'd crushed him with her little game. She couldn't possibly understand how hurt he was.

He'd fucked up and now his partner knew it. He'd broken the cardinal rule by getting involved with someone linked to his case, a person of interest. What would Darryl do with the information? Would he pull him from the case? It didn't matter. Either way, he'd still work it. He was going to see it through to the bitter end.

For Aimee.

Damn, did she have him twisted up.

"We haven't officially taken her off the suspect list," Darryl said.

"She's innocent."

For all of Aimee's faults, he at least believed that.

"For your sake, I hope you're right. She's seductive, manipulative, and deceitful. Do you know how many times I've caught her in a lie?"

"I know her personality. I admit there have been times when I've been unsure of my own thoughts, but I believe in her innocence. She's not a cold-blooded killer, and she's not the same woman. Her sister's murder has changed her."

As angry as he was with Aimee, he couldn't deny the change he'd seen and the pain in her eyes, as if she had the weight of the world on her shoulders.

"We've never been able to confirm Aimee's alibi for her sister's murder," Darryl said.

James frowned at the reminder. Aimee claimed she'd been at the club that night, but none of her employees had been able to confirm or deny it.

It annoyed him that he kept coming back to Aimee.

"Donovan called," Darryl added. "Marc Trevor was just rolled into the morgue, hours after I spoke to him."

"It wasn't Aimee."

Darryl groaned. "I'm not going to like her alibi, am I?"

"No. You're not."

"Christ, Hawke, I thought you were smarter than that. You willing to risk your career over this woman?"

His jaw clenched. Would he risk everything for Aimee, a woman who'd used him? If it was in pursuit of the truth, he knew the answer.

Yes. He would do the same for anyone.

"Aimee is innocent, like I said. Besides, it's not an issue. It's over."

Darryl focused pointedly on his clenched fists. "It may be stalled, but don't kid yourself. It's not over," he said, then changed the subject. "He's not our guy. Not only was his DNA not a match, but we've got surveillance footage which clearly shows him working during the estimated TOD. There was no way he could get to the club and back without his absence being noted."

"What about the guy at the club?"

"Maxwell Martin Brooks, attorney for the club. Married but currently estranged. No charges made on his credit card from the club, though it's possible Aimee didn't charge him."

"What about Nick and Dean's victim? Any indication she's part of this?"

"Unlikely. Manner of death is inconsistent. It appears we have two unrelated killers in the city."

Exhaustion tugged at James, both emotional and mental. "This doesn't make any sense. Did Trevor know something he shouldn't? Was he a blackmailer? We know he was innocent of Louisa's murder, so why was he killed?"

"The two cases are undoubtedly linked, although I find it strange that Trevor was killed just after I spoke with him," Darryl said. "It was almost like it was an afterthought, as if someone hadn't known about Trevor until I sought him out."

James shifted. Darryl had a valid point. Usually someone was shut up *before* the police had a chance to speak with them, not after. Unless Trevor hadn't told him everything, and the killer had gotten nervous.

"We're potentially looking at more victims. If it's revenge, or jealously. Even anger," James continued. "Perhaps one of Louisa's partners grew a little too attached? Someone Louisa couldn't interact with outside the confines of the club, someone Ruth Burnes would not approve of."

Darryl nodded. "We need to find the man she had sex with the night she died and any others she may have slept with." He rubbed at the back of his neck with his hand. "No one has come forward yet? I thought Aimee's employees were supposed to be loyal."

"They seem to be," James said. "They've all answered our questions as truthfully as I can make out. They haven't tried to protect Aimee or each other, and have in my opinion been extremely candid. I think if one of them knew who was with Louisa, they would say."

"Are you sure? These are people paid to fake it."

James frowned. "So, we're still in agreement it's one of the club's clientele?" he asked.

Darryl stretched his arms above his head and his bones cracked. "Yes," he said. "Aimee told me she isn't particularly picky when it comes to her clients. Add that to Louisa's special interests, and you've got trouble just waiting to happen."

"I agree. So what's the next move?"

"I'm waiting for Carmichael to arrange the subpoena for Aimee's client list."

Aidan Carmichael was the lead Prosecutor in the DPP—Director of Public Prosecutions—who James had learned Darryl had worked with previously. He'd been told Carmichael was a good man and an even better lawyer. He worked on the side of the victim and fought each case like it personally touched him.

"We've got DNA that belongs to a Daniel McGee, age thirty-eight," Amelia stated as she joined them, removing her jacket and tossing it over the back of her chair. "Am I interrupting something?"

She glanced between them, obviously sensing the tension.

"How'd his DNA end up in the system?" Darryl asked. "Career crim?"

She shook her head. "No, nothing like that. He's a P.I. Runs his business out of a shop on Charles Street."

Darryl's brow furrowed. "Aimee told me she had

each of her clients vetted using a private investigator."

"I believe McGee is that man. I looked into his financials and there are lots of charges from the club to his credit cards."

"Well, let's go ask him some uncomfortable questions."

Chapter 36

Daniel McGee was a hulk of a man who looked at home in black leather and chains. James didn't doubt that McGee rode around on a Harley, and he smelled of cigarettes and hard liquor. The man was a walking cliché, his inner voice sneered. He wasn't sure why, but he didn't like him. The man just rubbed him the wrong way and he hadn't even opened his mouth yet.

He looked annoyed, and there were multiple, long jagged scratches on his cheek that appeared painful and were beginning to form a scab. James wondered what happened to him.

"Looks like you came up against someone who didn't like you," he said, and received a grunt from McGee in return.

He gently touched the deep gouges. "Damn bitch. She wasn't a fan."

James gave him a cold hard stare, clearly stating he was not amused. Darryl unbuttoned his jacket and sat down across from McGee at the table. James was about to follow suit when he caught movement out the corner of his eye.

As he closed the door behind him, he heard Darryl begin the interview.

"Tell me about Louisa Burnes," he said.

"A fine piece of arse. Too bad what happened to her, but I can't say I'm surprised. She was a slut and we both know what happens to women like that."

James adjusted his tie and moved towards the gorgeous woman who was the bane of his existence, ignoring the conversation in the room.

"Aimee," he said.

She spun around, her ponytail almost whipping him in the face. He jerked slightly, his gaze running over her body until he focused on her face. She was an extremely beautiful woman and he never failed to notice. She wore a black skirt that reached mid-thigh, her long legs looking delectable in heels and encased in silk, making his mouth water. Her white fitted blouse covered her like a second skin and was tight across her breasts, outlining her impressive cup size. He closed his eyes for a brief moment, willing his body to cooperate, and cursed the fact that he was so attracted by her, to the point that she took over his thoughts completely.

"I came to talk to you."

"Now is not a good time."

"You've ignored my calls," she said.

There was a reason for that. "I'm busy."

"You're avoiding me."

"That too. I need to get back in there."

Her gaze turned to the door he indicated. Her eyes widened as she grasped the significance.

"You have a suspect?" Aimee asked, her eyes so

full of hope that he immediately snapped out of his lust-filled angry haze and began to think logically again.

He took a deep breath. "We have a person of interest."

"But he's someone involved in Louisa's life, right? The man she was with the night she died?"

"I can't comment."

"Please tell me, James. Do you think this is the person who killed my sister?"

On one hand, he wanted to tell Aimee they'd caught the man just to ease her suffering, but the cop in him didn't believe in discussing the case with anyone other than his partner and that extended to the victim's families.

"You're not going to tell me, are you?" she asked.

He sent her a pained look. "Aimee," he said softly, but the agony of knowing he'd hurt her was in clear in his voice.

"It's okay, I understand. I don't like it one bit but I understand."

"He's a person of interest," he said, choosing his words carefully. "Right now, we're tracking down his alibi. He looks good for this but that's just my opinion. We'll know more soon."

"Thank you," she said.

At that moment, the door to the interview room opened and Darryl along with Daniel McGee stepped through. Darryl shook his head at James to let him know that he believed they didn't have the right man.

Something inside him twisted painfully. He'd

done more than hope. He'd wished this case would come to an end, that they'd finally caught the son-of-a-bitch. Now he was sorely disappointed.

He turned at the sharp intake of breath to his left and found Aimee's pale face right before colour swamped her cheeks.

"You bastard," she hissed. As she started forward, James intercepted, blocking her path with his body. He caught her about the waist to hold her still. Aimee glared over his shoulder.

"Calm down, Aimee," he murmured in her ear. "We have no proof he's the killer, only circumstantial evidence."

Aimee cut him a glance before refocusing on McGee who flashed her a sly smile.

"Aimee, baby, good to see you again," he said.

"Drop dead, arsehole."

He winked at her. "Always a pleasure." He stopped beside her and whispered, "So was your sister."

She growled low in her throat and fought against him. At that very moment he believed she could've easily ripped out his throat if he hadn't been restraining her.

He sent McGee a warning look over Aimee's head. The private eye was already pushing the limit. He chose to ignore the warning and go for the heart where it would hurt the most.

"I must say she didn't have your expertise and style but what we did together eclipsed even your talents. I thank you for the introduction, after all, we shared mutual passions at your club. She had such energy and enthusiasm and enjoyed everything I did to her."

"You're nothing but scum who doesn't know the meaning of the word no."

His gaze burned a hole in McGee.

"Did he rape you?" James asked, his body stiff with barely restrained rage. His hold on Aimee tightened slightly as if he could protect her from the world. He knew he was too late for that. He was already too close to the case—to Aimee—but there was nothing he could do about that, not now. She'd crawled under his skin while he wasn't looking and burrowed deep into his heart and he knew he would kill to protect her. And if he couldn't kill, he could certainly maim and McGee was a lowlife he would gladly squash to relieve her of any further suffering.

She didn't take her gaze off McGee. "No," she said. "It didn't get that far. I wouldn't let it."

He let out a relieved breath. The idea McGee had forced himself on Aimee was something he couldn't bear. Just the knowledge that they'd slept together was enough to boil his blood with jealously and anger. He nodded curtly and pulled Aimee gently away, determined to put some distance between the P.I. and Aimee's simmering rage, which he had no doubt was about to erupt. He wasn't disappointed.

"If you killed her, I'll cut off your balls and ram them down your throat!" she told him in a tone that told everyone it was no idle threat.

"Hey, she just threatened me." McGee pointed at Aimee even as he glanced about the room at the officers going about their daily routine. "Is anyone going to do anything about that?"

They all stared at him.

"I see how it is. You're all blinded by a pair of tits. You want to talk to me again, you can go through my lawyer," he said and stormed out the room, swearing as he went.

Aimee turned to face him. "Do you believe he killed her?"

"He's on the top of the list but we have some investigating to do. All we know is he's the man Louisa was with prior to her death."

"From what we can determine, it was consensual," Darryl added.

"I had no idea he had the same sexual perversion as she did. If I had, I would've known long before now," Aimee said.

"You never saw them together at the club?" Darryl asked.

"No. I act as the hostess, making sure everyone's having a good time. It would have been easy to slip past me. I should've been a better sister to Louisa. I've let so much escape me, things that if I'd noticed, I could've prevented her death."

"You can't blame yourself, Aimee. People make their own decisions and where that leads is anyone's guess."

"If he killed her, we'll find out and he will be held accountable," Darryl said.

"Thank you. I know we've had our moments but you've treated me decently. I appreciate that."

"Just don't cross us, and we'll keep treating you decently," Darryl told her. "Lie and we'll became bastards. Now, let's go discuss your *relationship* with McGee and the near miss."

Chapter 37

Anger churned James's gut. He'd barely been able to sit through Aimee's recount of the night she'd spent with McGee. He knew exactly when it had been, his memory piecing together the turn of events. She'd sought solace in another man's arms because of him and their heated exchange. He hadn't meant to hurt her. Rage had his fists clenched as he recalled her teary phone call and her passionate plea for him to leave. If he'd known the events preceding the call he sure as hell would've met her in person, held her while she sobbed. No matter how pissed he was at her, she deserved better.

He'd wanted McGee to be guilty. Not only to ensure the man got what he deserved for what he'd done to Aimee, but to close the case for all involved. He fit nicely into the role.

"Traffic cameras don't lie, and McGee has a lead foot," Darryl said. "I admit I too was leaning toward him. He enjoys harming women too much."

"Is Ms. Burnes going to file a complaint against

him?" Matt Murphy asked, joining the conversation taking place in the small conference room just off the Pig Pen.

James shook his head. "No. She thinks it'll do no good with her reputation and the fact that he'd attacked her after consensual sex."

His stomach soured at the thought of her and McGee together. He tried to block out the mental image of her legs wrapped around the bastard's hips as he thrust inside her. His hand clenched into a fist as he fought to rid his mind of the unwelcome images.

He thought of what they'd shared not so long ago. It had been phenomenal. The best he'd ever had. He kept asking himself if it'd been her *talents*, as McGee had said, or if there'd been underlining emotions hidden in the actions. He couldn't seem to grasp a thought long enough to make sense of the emotional war going on inside him.

Matt nodded. "I think I'll poke around in McGee's affairs a little more. See if I can't rustle up some of his other previous partners."

The intention was clear.

"Good. That will at least get one more creep off the streets. Meanwhile, we're back to square one, without a suspect."

"You've cleared her, then? Unequivocally?" Matt asked. "She has the most to gain and to lose. Maybe she knew Louisa never stopped using her club for her sexual rendezvous? Or maybe she was jealous that McGee was sleeping with them both."

"Just the one time, and that was after Louisa's death," James clarified. He didn't like hearing

Aimee's reputation being dragged through the mud.

"So she says," Amelia added. "For all we know, they could've been banging each other for months."

"Aimee didn't kill her sister," he said, refusing to budge. He would never believe her guilty and not just because he had screwed her and wanted to do it again. He knew people and while Aimee was a hard one to read, his gut—not his dick—told him she was innocent.

"Where's your proof?" Darryl asked.

"Stop thinking with your little brain, Hawke, and start thinking with the one on top of your neck," Amelia added, and James glared at her.

Aimee didn't kill Louisa, couldn't have killed Trevor, and they were going on the surmise that his death was linked with hers. They'd done a brief check into his life and discovered that other than some serious credit card issues, the man led an uninteresting life surrounded by cars, odd jobs, and numerous women. The murder seemed off to him. He'd seen many crimes over the years and the various weapons used. Never once had he seen a car used to kill someone that way. But then, it could very well be a crime of opportunity. Why bring a knife to the party when you could just lower the jack?

"I am thinking," he said. "I just don't believe it. There isn't enough evidence to make me think otherwise."

Amelia scowled. "So what, Aimee Burnes needs to be standing over a dead body with a bloody butcher knife in her hand for you to believe?"

James scowled at her. She stared right back, but

he didn't flinch or back down. "Yes."

No way in hell was he about to back down. But he knew she had a point and he was the first to admit he'd gotten too close to Aimee over the course of the investigation. But a lot of things didn't add up and he wasn't about to let Aimee take the rap.

Darryl tapped his fingers against the table top. "Hawke's right. Unfortunately, we need more and I'm not about to arrest anyone without sufficient proof."

"Then go get her client list," Murphy said.

They disbanded, exiting the conference room. He stopped when he found Aimee sitting at one of the vacant desks.

"Can we talk?" she asked tentatively, standing.

Her ponytail fell over shoulder, curling over her breast, and his hand itched to free the long tresses.

He wanted to be stronger and demand she leave him alone. She'd messed with him enough. What more could she possibly want with him?

"I'm not sure we have anything more to say." He turned his back on her as he pretended to find interest in something behind him in hopes she'd get the hint and leave. He didn't want to do this now—especially not at the LAC with his colleagues just a few feet away.

Since she'd waited for forty minutes while they'd gone over the facts of the case he doubted she'd give up now. One way or another he was going to have to talk to her. Hadn't she done enough by ripping his heart out? He was afraid to talk. He was too angry and may say something he'd regret, even more than the last words he'd flung at her. He needed time to calm down.

"Well, I do," she said forcefully, coming to stand in front of him. The determination in her eyes momentarily stunned him before he took her arm and pulled her into the conference room.

When she gasped, he realised his mistake. The corkboard walls were covered in graphic pictures of Louisa and other pertinent information, including timelines and brief biographies of the major players. Aimee stared at the walls in silence. She focused on where they'd crossed out McGee's name.

"I was trying hard not to get my hopes up," she said. "I just want this to be over. Finally lay her to rest and forget about this whole ordeal. Like that would ever happen, right? It doesn't matter who murdered her, not really, because I share half the blame. I'm the one who introduced her to this lifestyle and it got her killed."

"People make their own choices, Aimee. Louisa was no different."

He crossed his arms over his chest and leaned against the rectangular Beechwood table, waiting for her to get on with why she was there, tormenting him with her presence. Even after all the shit that went down between them, he still wanted her.

She turned to him, her eyes bright with tears. "I was going to let you walk away without explaining my actions. But I can't. I won't. For the first time in my life, something means everything to me and I don't want you to believe the worst of me." She took a shaky breath. "I'm so sorry, James. I never meant to hurt you. Never meant to deceive you."

His heart was about to explode through his chest. "Then why did you?"

"Because I'm poison. Everything I touch, I ruin. You've changed me, made me want to be better and I changed you. I took what was good and crushed it. I just wanted you to find your way again."

She thought he'd lost his way? Shit, all his visits and she'd assumed he'd become a sex crazed nymphomaniac. Was the truth any better? He blamed her for lying to him but he was guilty of doing the same. Worse, if he thought about it, because his actions considered her a suspect which he knew in his heart not to be true. He was a damn bastard and she'd see it soon enough. Then all would truly be lost.

"I don't need saving, Aimee," he said, his words harsher than intended.

"I'm so sorry." Her voice broke and her lip trembled. She'd misunderstood his meaning. Was it any wonder the way he'd spoken to her?

"You shouldn't be the one to apologise. I was sent in undercover to watch the club. Anything I did there was purely to stay close and avoid detection," he admitted, feeling like the lowliest human being.

He waited for the pleading for forgiveness to die in her eyes.

Her face crumbled. She laughed, the sound shrill. "And you had the audacity to accuse *me* of games?"

"I was angry."

"And clearly I was stupid and naïve. Congratulations, James. I haven't had a man make a fool of me in years. You should be proud of yourself."

Her words cut into him better than any sharp knife, and he deserved each and every one of them. He'd broken her trust. Destroyed their tentative friendship in the span of a few minutes.

"I'm not."

"At least you're honest. Did you find what you were looking for?"

He kept his gaze on hers. "Yes," he replied. "You."

"I didn't kill my sister."

"I know. That's not what I meant. I'm forever saying the wrong thing around you." He moved toward her. Aimee backed up, putting space between them but he quickly crossed it and took her hand. She tried to pull it away but he held firm. He needed to make things right with her.

"I'm sorry, Aimee. I wish I could take back all the hurtful things I said." He remembered one word in particular and shuddered at the mistakes he'd made. He pulled her closer and wrapped his free arm around her waist. She remained stiff. "You're not poison. Please forgive me. I know I have no right to ask. I've made mistakes I don't deny that. But you're the best thing that's ever happened to me."

She eyed him warily. A vice squeezed his heart. He could see everything slipping away. He scrambled to pick up the pieces.

"Don't give up on me," he continued. "I want to be different than the other men in your life. I want to be the one that stays—the last one. I know I have to earn your trust and I promise you if you just give me a chance I'll prove to you that not all men are bastards."

"James," she said on a long exhale. Her body relaxed. He tightened his arm, savouring the feeling of just holding her for a minute before kissing her. He explored her mouth as if for the first time. For him, it really was, and the kiss tasted even sweeter than the last, hot and demanding. Full of passion, yet exquisitely slow and tender.

He was trembling by the time they pulled away. He rested his forehead against hers. He swallowed hard against the raw emotion raging inside him. He couldn't believe he'd almost lost this woman.

He pulled her closer into his arms, savouring the feel of her against him. She came willingly to him and his heart swelled.

Aimee. God, how he wanted and needed her. She was like the blood in his veins and the oxygen in the air. Without her, he would cease to exist. How did he get so tangled up?

He hadn't come looking for love but wasn't about to fight it either. He needed to know where he stood with her, if they could have a future together when this was all over. He knew he wasn't about to walk away. Did Aimee feel the same? He wanted to ask, but now was not the time. What they had was too new. Both had been burned in the past. Both had so much to overcome.

He held Aimee tight, both his arms around her waist while hers were secured around his neck. He would never give up on her on. Not now. Not ever. She was his.

"Thank you," he said, his voice barely above a whisper. He would treasure her gift for the rest of his life.

Chapter 38

For the first time in a good long while, Aimee had a bounce in her step. She was positively glowing. Tiffany had commented on that, and Aimee hadn't been able to stop smiling. She was glad she'd gone against her better judgement and sought James out. After the vile things he'd said to her, she should've left him alone, written him off like she had all the others, but Aimee had wanted to talk. Wanted him to understand why she hadn't been able to leave him alone.

Her heart skipped a beat at the memory of him telling her she was the best thing that had happened to him. She'd almost not believed him but the look in his eyes had her melting. She wasn't sure how to feel about that but hope blossomed deep down inside her that maybe, just maybe, they had a chance. If she could love anyone, it would be James.

Love.

She was already half in love with him. Her breathing quickened when she saw him and her stomach fluttered and her heart ached when they were separated. Could he possibly love her? Surely it was much too soon for that, but then she'd already accepted that she was on her way there. Speeding toward the feeling without concern over the consequences. She felt reckless. She'd never risked her heart like this before. But deep down, Aimee believed she could trust him.

Something had changed within her, shifted and it wasn't just the sex, which was the most gratifying experience of her life. She'd connected with James and her heart had broken when he'd walked out on her. She never wanted to feel like that again. Once Aimee would never have let a man have so much power over her. Now, she didn't mind so much. She felt lighter and dare she think it—happier?

Except when she dwelled on Louisa.

Who had killed her and why?

The police believed it to be someone linked to her club. She'd been right; she had killed her sister. She hadn't wielded the knife, but she was morally responsible.

She would never forgive herself.

Aimee sat back in her office chair, lost to the past. If only she could redo her life. Start from scratch. There were so many things she would do differently or in most cases not at all. But then there was James. Sweet, loving James. What he saw in her, she had no idea. Besides the sexual, she didn't think she had much to offer. Could she even entertain the idea of spending time with him? She didn't want to mar him with her presence, suddenly feeling unclean and unworthy.

Why James? Her brain screamed.

Why did her heart have to fall for such a sweet simple man, a man who was unlike anyone else? A man who sent her heart racing and her libido sky-rocketing. Just the memory of how they were together was enough to get her wet and more than ready.

She was beyond tired. The situation regarding Louisa had drained her and guilt consumed her at not calling her mother. She couldn't stand the woman but if Aimee was feeling like this over losing a sister, what was her mother feeling losing her daughter? It didn't matter that her mother was a class-A bitch. She had loved Louisa in her own way. Of course, there was no love lost for Aimee, but she had finally come to terms with that. It didn't matter anymore. Life was too short for grudges and reliving the past. Even as much as she wanted to change things, she couldn't, and had to live with her choices.

Did her mother have regrets at not loving her daughters completely? At allowing her husband, the father of her children, to walk out the door? Her mother had never told them the circumstances of his abandonment and Aimee doubted she'd ever learn the reason her father had left. Had it been her mother, had she been too hard to live with? Aimee could understand that. She, too, had walked out the door and never looked back. To this day, she hadn't stepped foot inside her mother's house. Not since she was kicked out twelve years earlier.

Had her father been an adulterer? She knew her mother wouldn't have abided that. Not only was it a sin but even Ruth had her pride. Had her mother forced him to go like she had Aimee? Being of the Catholic faith, divorce wouldn't have been an option for Ruth and she would've rather died first than admit failure.

Aimee sighed. There were no answers. Would she die with those very questions on her lips? What was a normal life like? Hell, she wouldn't know if it came up and bit her on the arse.

Up until a few days ago, she had thought her life complete. Meeting James had made her yearn for things she'd never considered.

His body hard and strong. She remembered that body and how it had felt beneath her. He was a man of strength, comforting and caring, all rolled into one package and she didn't deserve it.

But damn did she want it.

***

James followed Darryl into Aimee's club at a much slower pace, working things through his mind. He'd walked into the LAC, feeling the happiest he'd ever been, the emotion rapidly evaporating when all eyes had turned his way. He'd known something bad was coming his way by the looks of pity and sympathy thrown in his direction. His first thought was something had come from the client list. He recalled the words that had shaken him to the core.

"The blood sample they found under Louisa's fingernails...Stone got the results from his preliminary test and says the blood is female and closely related to Louisa."

His heart had stopped, his breath catching in his throat. *Aimee*.

He refused to believe it, despite the evidence against her. He had to figure out a way to help her. But since he hadn't discovered the identity of the real murderer in the past few days, he doubted he would in the next three minutes, but he raced to come up with a motive or opportunity. Aimee was looking far too good for this. He knew if he didn't come up with an answer, Aimee would be spending her life behind bars.

She smiled when she saw them. Her long hair hung loose down her back, in soft waves. Her eyes were outlined with dark eyeliner, bringing out the unique almond shape and her lips were red.

She wore dark stressed jeans that hugged her hips and thighs and a pair of Adidas sneakers. Her delicious chest was encased in a sky blue square neck shirt with quarter length sleeves which covered her upper body like a second skin. Did she own any other kind? A sparkle caught his eye and he noticed she had a gold chain around her neck, an A done in diamonds which matched her stud earrings hung from a loop on the chain. James's heart squeezed and he wished he wasn't there. But he was a cop, and personal relations don't—or shouldn't—get in the way.

It was too late. He'd held Aimee in his arms all night, her back pressed against his chest as he spooned her. They'd both worn clothes, his unbearably tight in the groin area. He'd suffered through. Sex was not everything and certainly not what he wanted most. He wanted to cherish Aimee. Show her that men were more than just dicks. So after they left the conference room he'd followed her back to the club to get her client list and after forwarding it to Darryl, he'd taken Aimee home and put her to bed, wrapping her gently in his arms and held her. She'd melted into him and he knew he surprised and amazed her. He was glad. He wanted to be different from all those who'd come before him. She'd broken down, a tidal wave of pain released as she clung to him. Her words fragmented broken by sobs.

Finally, hours later, she'd relaxed.

"Detectives," Aimee said, and James tried not to notice the bounce in her step and the life in her eyes. She looked so utterly beautiful it was a physical pain to him. He had never seen Aimee so happy, so free. She wasn't a businesswoman this morning, nor was she a lover, she was just Aimee Burnes—the real Aimee Burnes, the one he hadn't had a chance to meet. The carefree and jubilant woman who had been squashed before she'd a chance to rise. James cursed silently. Aimee glanced from Darryl to him and then back to Darryl, her gaze never staying on him for long.

"Have you got news?"

Darryl gave her his cop face. Emotionless. As if the outcome of the day didn't matter at all. But James knew it did, had seen deep down that Darryl had doubts, had seen him melt towards Aimee. But the evidence was pointing to her and they had no other suspects. Right now he hated his job. James closed his eyes as the Darryl spoke.

"Aimee Burnes, you are under arrest." Darryl said, reciting her rights.

Her expression seemed to say she was waiting for the punch line.

"What? You're arresting me? You've got to be kidding." But she still stepped back, away from Darryl, and James could feel her gaze on him, boring into his skin.

"Please put your hands behind your back, Ms. Burnes."

"Detective Hill?" She stared at James in shock when she realised he wasn't kidding. "James? What? I…I don't understand."

James cringed at the sound of her voice, so lost. So frightened. It took everything he had not to pull her into his arms. But he couldn't. His hands became fists beside his thighs.

"Ms. Burnes…Aimee…please." Darryl's voice was soft, pleading. Obviously not liking this anymore than James.

Aimee immediately put her hands behind her back and Darryl handcuffed her.

"W-why?" she asked. "Please tell me why."

James spoke up, finding his voice. "We found your blood on the body of Louisa Burnes."

Aimee's gaze found his and he flinched. Gone was the joyful woman happy to see him. In her place was a confused and scared woman, the fear in her eyes heartbreaking. "My blood? How did my blood get on Louisa?"

"That's what we want to know, Ms. Burnes. Let's go," Hill said as he led Aimee out the door of her club and over to the waiting Commodore.

Chapter 39

Aimee had never been in an interview room before but it looked just like it did in the movies. She nervously bit her bottom lip and settled into the uncomfortable seat.

This is bad. This is really fucking bad.

The charge was murder. The sentence may as well be life. By the time she got out, she would be old enough for retirement. How could they think she could kill her own sister? She stared at the two-way mirror. Who was on the other side? Was it James? Was he trying to help her? She instantly dismissed that idea. He couldn't help her. Only a solicitor could help her now unless the real killer showed up and confessed.

Did James believe her to be guilty? He hadn't said any reassuring words to her since she'd gotten in the police car and they'd driven to the LAC. But then could he? Was he even allowed to talk to her? She had just been arrested for murder. Surely he would need to distance himself from her. She could only imagine what would happen to his career if it got out that he had a personal relationship with a suspect. She hoped he didn't get into trouble. He was too good of a man and she didn't deserve him. How could she have stupidly allowed herself to think they could have a future together?

Her gaze drifted to the small camera overhead recording her every move for review later. The microphone was screwed to the middle of the table so no one could be tempted to use it as a weapon against the detectives who'd be doing the interviewing. The door opened and she jumped, admitting to herself that she was frightened.

Darryl sat down across from her and identified himself, James, and her for the recording along with the time and date as James joined him on the other side of the table. He would always be on the other side, and if he let her, she would drag him down. She wasn't about to allow that. He deserved a woman who hadn't been arrested for murder, who didn't have such a dark and dishonourable past.

Aimee rubbed her palms over her arms and shook slightly. Fear was becoming an unwelcome friend. The room wasn't cool, but knowing why she here made her uneasy. She had never been this terrified in her entire life.

James must've noticed her shivering because in the next minute he asked if she wanted a cup of coffee or something. She shook her head, not looking at him, afraid he would see her crumbling. Whatever happened to her shouldn't have any effect on him. She was already on the verge of tears and it was taking her entire willpower not to let the tears flow, but she had experience in not showing her emotions and she would damn well use that fact to her advantage if she could help it. The whole thing felt like a nightmare—a bad fucking nightmare, and all she wanted to do was wake up and have Louisa back.

"You think I killed my sister?"

Terror had her heart thumping. He thought she'd killed Louisa. Surely, he knew her better than that. Maybe he did. She could be manipulating, controlling, cold. Darryl had more than one reason to believe her capable of stabbing her sister.

"Why not? We have enough evidence," Detective Hill said.

She kept her gaze on him. She couldn't bring herself to look at James and have him see the shame, disgust, or hate in his eyes for what she was. He could no longer turn a blind eye to the woman he'd screwed and been screwed by.

"She was my sister."

"Where were you the night Louisa was murdered?"

"I told you. I was at my club."

Detective Hill shook his head. "We checked with your employees. Not one of them admitted to seeing you there."

Her heart beat faster as she got caught in her lie. The truth was her saviour, and her condemner all in one. Her skin was damp with nervous sweat as she twisted her hands tightly together.

"I wasn't working. I was in one of the rooms."

Hill's eyebrow rose. "Were you alone?"

She nibbled at her lip and swallowed hard at the knot in her throat. She contemplated at what to say.

She should've just told the truth from the beginning but then they would have believed her to be the killer without proof, without knowing her and seeing there was more to her than her external shell.

God, how did she get into this mess?

If she explained everything, maybe they would pass over it if they decided it had no bearing on the case. Could she risk it? The moment she told the truth, it would be on record.

No, she couldn't tell them. Aimee Burnes might be a lot of things, but a destroyer wasn't one of them and someone's life would be completely fucked up if she spoke.

Her thoughts must have shown on her face. "The truth, Ms. Burnes," Detective Hill said.

She rocked slightly in her chair, fighting the tears. It wasn't every day she faced murder charges.

She shook her head. "No," she said, the word almost inaudible.

"No? So who were you with?" Hill continued the questioning, and Aimee could feel James's gaze boring into her. She refused to look at him.

"A friend," she said, steel in her backbone, her teeth clamped together. She needed to start protecting herself. She knew she was innocent and it was their job to find out who wasn't. She hadn't done anything illegal and didn't want to be treated as if she had.

"A client?"

She glared at the detective. "I don't fuck my clients!"

Aimee darted a guilty look at James, because they'd fucked when he had technically been a client, or at least she had thought him to be. It had been true, up until she'd had sex with James.

She might work in a sex club, but she wasn't a whore. She may not have been as picky about her bed partners in the past as she should've been, but she was not for sale. Never had been, and never would be.

She at least had her honour, not that anyone would believe her. She'd always been unfairly judged.

"So tell me his name and we can get you out of here."

She shook her head. "I can't do that."

Detective Hill waited for a response, then said, "Why not?"

James huffed loudly. "Oh, for fuck's sake, Aimee, just give us his name."

She darted a surprised look at him and wished she hadn't. His face was flushed from his outburst and his light eyes were angrier than she'd ever seen. She had the sudden urge to be somewhere else, away from him.

"He's married. I can't do that to him."

Max had been a friend since she'd first opened Club X, and had given her support and suggestions when she had no one to turn to. He was a successful attorney, and she had taken his advice and turned her life around. She had caught him on the worst night of his life. Drunk, he had allowed Jenna to seduce him, and regretted the desperate decision as his life crumbled around him. He told her he'd fucked up and needed a friend.

She had spent the night talking him down off a

ledge, but she doubted anyone would believe there'd been no sex involved. Least of all his wife, who was the jealous kind. Margie had never approved of their friendship. Max loved his wife and would die if she left him.

"I see. How honourable you are," Detective Hill said.

"I don't care what you think of me," she replied, but she did care what *James* thought of her. She darted another look at him, wanting to explain, unable to bear him looking at her in a whole new light.

"You should."

They were interrupted when the door to the interview room opened. A female cop stood there, Ruth Burnes beside her.

What the hell was her mother doing here? She entered the room like a queen, her gaze surveying Aimee, her lip curled in distaste.

"Wipe that stuff off your face," Ruth ordered before facing Detective Hill.

Aimee brought up her hand, and using the sleeve of her blouse, attempted to wipe off her make-up. Normally, she would've told her to go jump, but the fact that her mother was standing there in the room with her made her heart swell, the tears threatening to return.

She had never thought her mother gave a moment of thought toward her. Aimee was comforted knowing that even though she disapproved of her daughter, when the chips were down, Ruth had come through.

"Detective Hill, I know my daughter didn't kill

her sister. Aimee wouldn't hurt Louisa. Besides, my daughter has an alibi, however dishonourable." Once again, she frowned in disgust. "And apart from a blood sample that could have come from anywhere, you have nothing."

"You want us to release her?"

The woman cop spoke up, her dark hair neatly tied back into a ponytail, her slacks and shirt ironed. "No, of course not, Detective Hill. But the superintendent has agreed to release Aimee into Mrs. Burnes's custody until formal charges are filed."

Aimee's eyes widened. Her mother had never done anything nice for her before, and here she was offering to get her out of a night in jail and possibly many more. All it took was for her beloved daughter to be murdered and her remaining daughter to be arrested for murder.

"That can be arranged, Mrs. Burnes," Detective Hill said.

Ruth nodded. "Thank you, Detective. Come along, Aimee."

She jumped from her seat, an overwhelming urge to hug her mother coming over her, and without thinking she did just that. Ruth let out an *oomph* as Aimee held her close. The tears that had threatened to overtake her began rolling down her cheeks. "Thank you for coming." She sobbed as Ruth extradited herself from Aimee's grasp.

"What else was I to do? Now, we must move along. You've completely messed up my schedule," Ruth snapped.

Aimee didn't care. She was getting out of there,

away from murder, away from people who believed the worst of her, away from everything. She would take the downtime to seriously review her life—and change it.

"I didn't sleep with him. I know you probably don't believe me, but it's true," she said. "I just can't drag him into this."

She couldn't face James but she needed to tell him that much. She couldn't stand that he of all people would look at her with distaste, regretting the passion they shared.

She turned and obediently followed Ruth out the door without one glance back at the detectives. Hope danced across her mind and she knew she had been given a second chance, and she wasn't about to blow it.

Chapter 40

Aimee had never liked her mother's house, only thinking of it as Ruth's home. Never hers. Never the Burnes house, just Ruth's. The house was something to be admired to be sure. Everything had its special spot and everything had a purpose and Aimee knew Louisa had adopted her mother's strange habit. Aimee's gaze fell on the white porcelain angels standing on the side table and remembered how many times her mother had gotten angry when Aimee had touched one.

Little girls were for admiring and were never supposed to be dirty which Aimee had often been, much to Ruth's dismay. Ruth Burnes had raised her girls to be perfect. Not a hair was to be out of place and no smudge was to mar their pretty faces. Their church dresses were to be ironed and clean and it drove Aimee crazy.

Children were to be seen, not heard, part of Ruth's Rules and Regulations which Aimee had called the constant dos and don'ts her mother routinely came up with. She remembered being made to pray in front of the Virgin Mary before bedtime and to seek forgiveness for each action Ruth had deemed a sin.

Aimee wasn't very religious. She never had been despite being raised until the age of sixteen as a devout Catholic. She wanted to believe in God, but from the amount of shit that had happened in her short life, she figured if he did exist he owned her an explanation. A damn good one, at that.

Her father had left when she'd been a baby. Aimee understood, because even she hadn't wanted to live with her mother. She blamed Ruth for that, even though she hadn't heard the full story. Maybe her father was just a prick. Maybe he had been abusive and they'd been far better off without him, although she didn't believe it. Somewhere deep inside her she wanted to believe her father had been a decent man. Where was he now? No decent man left his daughters, even if he couldn't stand his wife.

Psychologists would've said her father abandoning her had a direct result on her love life, and they were probably right. It was hard to understand a loving relationship when you had nothing to base it on.

Ruth emerged from the kitchen with a bowl full of soup and Aimee blinked in surprise. At least her mother was trying.

It had been a strange day, and it wasn't over yet.

"Here you go," Ruth said, placing the pink and yellow floral design bowl on a placemat on the table.

"Thanks," Aimee said. Some things were ingrained. Her stomach growled.

James.

The sadness inside her bubbled to the surface, but that ship had sailed. Even if he was stupid enough to still want her, she wasn't about to ruin his life just for good sex—okay, great sex. Really fantastic, mind-blowing, name forgetting sex. For once in her life she wasn't going to manipulate someone because it suited her and her needs. No, she would let him go, if he wasn't gone already.

There was no such thing as a happy ending. Especially not for people like her. How many times had her mother told her she was going to Hell? At this moment, Aimee even welcomed it. She glanced over at the dark stained mahogany side table. A smiling and polished Louisa smiled at her. Standing beside her in a picture, her sweet, perfect older sister was dressed as usual in her Sunday best. Aimee remembered they'd just come from church, the white fabric of their dresses pressed and their shoes polished. It was the only way Ruth would take a photo. Nothing was ever spontaneous, no catching of a moment shared by two people. No sweet memory of how it had been as children, completely at ease. Everything was planned to smallest detail—what they would wear, how they would stand, and where the sun would be.

Aimee's gaze drifted around the room. Every photo of her and Louisa as kids looked like something out of a magazine, completely unreal as if they were mannequins in a store, their smiles forced and the happiness on their faces fake as they posed for the picture.

Aimee turned from the photos of her and Louisa

that adorned every surface. Something didn't sit well with her regarding the pictures, but she couldn't place the source of the unease. Her mother would've been better off with two Barbie dolls instead of daughters.

Aimee took her seat at the table and picked up the spoon, blowing on the soup before swallowing it. Ruth frowned before her chin rose and Aimee thought she was probably apologising to God for her daughter's lack of manners at forgetting to say Grace before her meal.

"I can't believe this," Ruth said. "One daughter murdered and another accused of killing her sister. What did I do to deserve this?"

Aimee was instantly contrite. Her mother wasn't all that bad, was she? She just had some really annoying quirks and maybe as Aimee had learned to harden her heart, her mother had also. It couldn't have been easy for her to raise two children by herself. God knows they'd had no family around them to provide support.

Maybe Ruth had treated them the only way she knew how. Aimee had never met her grandparents but maybe they had been just as cool towards their children as Ruth had been.

"I'm sorry, Mother," she said, and she meant it.

"That doesn't do a lot of good, does it?"

Aimee resisted the urge to roll her eyes. Well, there goes *that* sympathy.

"Is anything I ever say or do enough?"

Ruth gave a long suffering sigh as Aimee continued to gobble up the tasty soup. Her mother was a fantastic cook, and it was the one nice memory Aimee had growing up, her favourite time of the day. When Ruth had been mad at Aimee, she had sent her to bed without supper, knowing that would punish her more than anything else. Every meal was like eating in a restaurant, her mother planning everything down to the minute, but the result was nothing less than perfection.

"Don't make this out to be something it's not," Ruth said. "My poor Louisa was murdered." She made the sign of the cross over her chest.

Aimee couldn't believe it. She made it sound like Aimee had done something intentionally.

"And that's my fault?" she asked incredulously. It was finally becoming too much for her to handle. So much for the truce. "Mother, I hate to break it to you, but Louisa wasn't this innocent Virgin Mary you think she was. She came to my club every single night."

"Because you made her!" Ruth screamed.

Aimee shook her head. As much as she didn't want to hurt her mother, Ruth needed a harsh reality lesson. "I did no such thing. She came on her own volition and if not my club, she would've been walking into someone else's. And that's not all. She liked the hard stuff. Sex games, men whipping her body, strangling her, fuck—"

Ruth interrupted her, shrieking, "Stop it!"

"Do you still think her an angel?"

She had gone too far. Her mother wouldn't be able to take the overload to her system, and the shock could prove fatal. But her mother had always put her on edge and made her speak without thinking.

Ruth pinned her with a hateful look. "You are *both* whores!"

Aimee didn't blink. She had expected as much from her pious mother. "And you're a prude."

Aimee got up from the table, the soup half gone, her appetite completely dissipated. She started towards the stairs, ready to confine herself in her room as she had done years ago when her mother was raging.

"I know only too well," her mother yelled. "You have disgraced your family. It kills me to call you my daughter!"

Aimee swung around, standing at the bottom of the staircase. All the emotions she had bottled up inside her, years of suffering in silence, bubbled to the surface. "And it kills *me* to call you my mother! I guess we both lucked out," Aimee added with slightly more hate in her voice than her mother had before heading upstairs.

Her bedroom was her sanctuary in this house. She might've been better off in jail. Spending the next few days or weeks locked inside this prison with her mother would prove challenging at best. Would she make it? If the thought of never leaving didn't terrify her so much she would've called Detective Hill and begged him to lock her away.

How had she arrived here? She had gone from contentment with her life to being on the cusp of a murder conviction. She felt so utterly and completely alone and wanted nothing more than to run into James's open and comforting arms. Never going to happen. Not now, not ever. They were just too damn different and as much as she wanted to believe love could conquer all, she knew she was kidding herself. He was a cop and they were at an impasse.

Aimee pulled herself away from her depressing thoughts and back to reality. Had Ruth changed her room? She'd decorated it years before her departure. Had her mother removed her Hanson brothers' poster? She'd had a giant crush on Taylor along with a few others. The walls of her bedroom had been covered from ceiling to floor with cut-outs of everything she knew would piss her mother off and a few just because she liked them.

No, Ruth wouldn't have touched a thing. That would've required her to open the door to the room of the daughter she had never understood and could never bond with. Not that she'd tried.

Aimee looked forward to lying down on the blue-black quilt of her bed, suddenly tired, catching sight of the door to her bedroom only a few feet down the hall. She'd had boys in her room and listened to the devil's music, which her mother had called anything that wasn't a hymn. Lost in memories, she suddenly doubled over.

Aimee took deep breaths, willing her stomach to behave. Her head spun and she used the wall to ground her. She straightened, her limbs growing heavy, her mind threatening to go dark. She took a step towards her room, then another. When the truth sank in, Aimee almost collapsed to the carpeted floor.

Her mind struggled to make sense of it even as her body betrayed her.

"Rohypnol," she whispered, and sensed the

presence of someone behind her.

Chapter 41

James refused to believe Aimee was capable of murder. He knew her better than anyone did, and there was no way he could've been so blind.

What if you're wrong? A voice whispered in his mind.

Questions rose and he couldn't fight them. He hated that he'd suspected her, especially considering he'd been so adamant about her innocence not so long ago, but Darryl was right. Aimee was deceitful and had proven she had a spiteful side.

But also a kind one.

He wanted to be certain that not a single trace of doubt filled him, but he couldn't. Aimee had lied. Yet, he couldn't believe what they shared was a lie. And if he believed that, why couldn't he believe everything else?

Aimee had changed. She was not the manipulative woman he'd met at the mixer, and she wanted him. Her eyes couldn't lie, and neither did her grief. But had she changed too late?

She couldn't explain the blood, and her alibi couldn't be confirmed without her assistance, and it appeared she'd rather go to prison than betray a friend. Again, an admirable trait, though the idea of her protecting a man had jealously curling its ugly fingers into a hard fist in his belly.

Why the hell was this so complicated?

He caught the pitying looks his colleagues sent out the corner of his eye. That bothered him, but it was hardly the main emotion surging through him.

What must Aimee think?

He hadn't seen or spoke with her since she'd left with her mother. Was she rejoicing that she'd cheated punishment for now, or crying at what could be seen as his betrayal of her? His indecision over her innocence should hurt her. He wasn't sure which one he preferred. He should be comforting her. Telling her everything would be all right. Instead he remained at his desk, his thoughts warring.

Despair blossomed until he was sure it emanated from his pours. His first case as a detective and he'd messed up royally. Worst of all, he wasn't sure if he could recover, or if Aimee would ever forgive him. In such a short while, she'd turned his whole world upside down.

He wanted to believe her, but the evidence against her was too strong. He hoped she kept her freedom, if only to enjoy this new solidarity between mother and daughter. An interesting turn. It would seem Ruth wanted to reconnect with her remaining child, and he was glad, for Aimee's sake. Hopefully, it would ease some of the pain inside her.

She was the first suspected murderer he'd ever wished good things for.

Seriously messed up.

Doubt clouded his judgment. Was he truly going to ignore evidence over her words? She'd lied to him before. Had manipulated him. She was a master. He couldn't help but look back over everything she'd said, analysing every action. Had everything she'd said and done simply been a distraction to knock him off balance? Had she seduced him to keep him from looking too closely?

He recalled her passionate words. *For the first time in my life, something means everything to me.*

Had that too been a lie? He'd believed that to be an admission of her feelings, but he'd been the one to offer his heart. He'd been the one to beg her to give him a chance, to promise her that she could count on him. She'd given nothing in return, except her body, which he knew she gave freely and indiscriminately.

He second guessed himself, and Aimee.

He tried to call her and listened as it went to voicemail. A fist tightened in his gut. She was ignoring his call. Had she finally given up the game or was she trying to distance herself from him so he wasn't on the receiving end of any fall-back?

The latter pissed him off. She had to be innocent.

Wishful thinking.

Conflicted, he hung his head.

"Aimee not taking your calls?" Darryl asked from the desk beside him. His clothes were rumpled, having been in with the prosecutor of the case for over two hours, asking for more time. There were still questions to be answered.

"No."

Movement flickered in his peripheral vision and he turned as Doctor Stone approached, a frown on his face. "I've got the results on that blood sample."

His body went numb, as if to protect him. It was all over now.

"So it's conclusive, then?" he asked.

Stone shook his head. "I'm not sure. There's something strange with the sample. Something my preliminary test didn't detect."

Amelia leaned forward. "Contaminated?"

"No, nothing like that."

"What does it matter? We already know that it's Aimee's."

"Is that the young lady you arrested?"

James nodded.

Stone removed his glasses and began cleaning the lenses with a handkerchief he'd retrieved from his pocket. "Then it can't be hers," he said. "Not unless this Aimee suffers from aplastic anaemia."

"Aplastic anaemia?" Darryl asked.

Amelia interlocked her fingers. "Isn't that a sort of blood disease?"

"Very good, Detective Donovan. It is indeed."

The blood rushed from his face. "Aimee," he said, his voice laced with fear as he grabbed his weapon from his drawer.

Chapter 42

Aimee used all her strength to stay vertical, her body weighing her down and darkness threatened to swamp her. She bit her lip to keep from going under, tasting the coppery tang of blood. What was happening? The memory returned as she fought the haze in her head. She'd been drugged. Rohypnol—the rapist's drug of choice. Every woman's worst nightmare.

How? When? Was this the way Louisa had felt before she'd been stabbed, like she was drifting slowly into unconsciousness without any semblance of control?

Aimee imagined Louisa lying dead in the alley, blood spilling from her body, and she shivered. Panic swelled inside of her and made her heart thump. She didn't want to die, not now, and she fought to clear her mind. Where was she? What was she doing? Simple questions she couldn't answer.

Her mouth was dry and Aimee yearned for a drink to quench the thirst. Her stomach rolled, sick with fear. The black interceded on her consciousness, pulling her deeper into the dark. She wanted to lie down, to rest her heavy eyelids, but she knew she wasn't safe.

She sensed another's presence nearby and her eyes opened wide, the hair at the nape of her neck rising. Everything around her sounded so clear. The creak of the wood behind her as a body moved closer. The tick of the clock on the wall and the rustle of the curtains nearby as the wind blew the fabric away from the window. Aimee knew she was going to die. She, like Louisa would die alone and suddenly Aimee wanted to cry. She wished for nothing more than strong, loving arms to wrap around her and hold her, to be safe in the warm embrace of someone who cared for her. But she was Aimee Burnes and she had no one. She turned towards Louisa's killer.

"Mum?" she asked.

Ruth stood in front of her, an odd look on her face that changed her entire demeanour. The Ruth Burnes she'd always known was gone and in her place was a woman who had killed her daughter. She raised a frying pan above her head, the frail sickly woman's strength doubling, and brought the pan down on Aimee, glancing off the top of her head and the backs of her hands as Aimee brought them instinctively up. She fell to the floor, dazed and injured. Her head spun, pounding in response to the Teflon coated whack she'd just received, and that was when the oddness of the photos downstairs dawned on her.

She and Louisa were young girls. Always young. Forever trapped in adolescence when they had been innocent. Her mother had kept them locked away in her mind as pure young ladies, the kind a mother could be proud of. Aimee swallowed back the nausea, her hair and face sticky with blood that trickled down from the cut on her forehead.

"You're making me do this, you little slut," Ruth said.

"Mum?" she asked, unable to truly believe her mother would do this to her—to Louisa. What had happened to that commandment her mother had promised not to break?

Thou shall not kill.

"You and your sister were such filthy little harlots," Ruth said, her voice strange and distant, unlike anything Aimee had ever heard before. Ruth hit her with the frying pan again, getting Aimee in the side of the head.

A buzzing filled her ears. She trembled. Death wasn't too far away. If Ruth had killed her beloved Louisa, what hope was there for Aimee?

"Where were you when I needed you? Don't you think I wish things had gone differently?" Aimee asked. If only her mother had given her love and protection like she had Louisa, she might not have ended up screwing the first man who'd shown her the slightest affection. She might not have rebelled against her mother and her rules.

Ruth advanced on Aimee again, her eyes filled with hate and disgust. This is what Louisa had seen, what she had run from. Had she envisioned the devil coming forth, or was this really what her mother looked like? Right now Aimee couldn't remember Ruth looking like anything but the anger filled woman descending on her.

Run, Aimee, move!

She screamed at herself or was it Louisa who was yelling at her? Filled with a muscle relaxant and hypnotic sedative, she wasn't sure, and frankly didn't care. If her sister was telling her to move, who was she to argue? She was only too happy there was someone on her side, someone who cared whether she lived or died.

Aimee's knuckles stung from the blow of the frying pan but she ignored the pain as she slid on her buttocks away from Ruth. The carpet beneath her bum burned her jeans as it made contact, causing friction. The heels of her sneakers pushed at the floor, helping her to put distance between them.

Never once had she considered her mother could've killed Louisa or even attempt to hurt her. All the years her mother got angry she took it out in words and emotional torture, never physical. But Aimee knew Ruth had killed Louisa, had taken a knife and had stabbed her older sister repeatedly, and she'd gotten away with it too. No one would have ever believed Ruth Burnes of harming her daughters.

Ruth the devout Catholic would never do such a thing, and the police hadn't even considered her a suspect. Anger bubbled inside her. They had practically accused Aimee from day one, no matter what she said to assure them otherwise. She had helped them with whatever enquiry they had, but it wasn't enough, and now she was going to pay the price for their narrow-mindedness.

Aimee Burnes would die a horrible death. She

could see the newspaper reports: *Sex club owner brutally murdered.*

Well, at least then I'll be exonerated, she thought, as a wave of hysteria overtook her.

Chapter 43

Ruth stared down at her daughter, the harlot, the jezebel that had ruined her life and knew she was doing the right thing. For years, she'd distanced herself, wanting to be rid of Aimee. She'd wanted nothing to do with the whore but God was supposed to love all, even the sinners. But try as she might, she had never felt anything for her younger daughter, and then like a bad dream she had watched her sweet, darling Louisa take the path of the tainted, led by the daughter of Eve.

Her daughter.

How could God do this to her? Why had she bore the one who would remove her daughter from God's loving embrace?

What had she done to be handed the life she'd been given? From the moment she had married *that* man, she knew she'd made a horrible mistake. She was not a wife, not made for anything but to serve Him. She would've been happy in a convent living a life devoted to the Holy Father. But life hadn't cared what she wanted.

If it hadn't been for Louisa, she would've gone crazy, but she had looked into her sweet, innocent daughter's face and knew she was all that her little girl had, knew she had to protect her, to keep her away from the dirtiness in the world.

She hadn't wanted that man, her husband, to touch her, but it had been her wifely duty.

Aimee had been trouble even before she had been born, giving Ruth pain after pain, making sure she knew she was there, that her father had planted his unwanted seed in her. Ruth had even tried for an abortion, arranging accident after accident, but Aimee hadn't wanted to die. She'd fought for her life both times Ruth had *accidentally* fallen down the stairs. From birth, she was a constant reminder of her father. Where Louisa had the temperament of Ruth, Aimee had Steven's stubborn, strong-willed arrogance.

She'd been happy to ignore her younger daughter, had rejoiced when Aimee had left home after Ruth had found out she was no longer pure. She thanked God Louisa was out of harm's way, away from Aimee's influence. It had been a complete shock to discover Louisa had gone to Aimee's club and enjoyed God knows what there. Just the thought of the degrading, horrible, unclean things one did in those types of establishments made Ruth see red.

She'd hadn't meant to spy on her daughter, but after too many missed visits and evasive phone calls Ruth had become suspicious, so she had followed Louisa. She'd been so happy her daughter was so pure, thankful she had no man in her life, but that was when she'd learned the disgusting truth. She had almost keeled over when she's seen her beloved Louisa walk into that building and not leave until hours later, coming out stinking of sex.

Pleasures of the flesh. Ruth scrunched up her face in disgust. She had never believed Louisa could've been led so easily astray. It hadn't worried her about Aimee. She had expected that from her, had always known she would come to a bad end. But having the truth of Louisa, the fraud who promised and pledged one thing only to do another, slapped in her face. Then something had snapped inside her mind and she had planned to rid the world of her daughters and anyone who had helped bring on their demise. Her years of anger watching her little girls descend into the gates of Hell to lay with the serpent was no longer bearable.

"You got what you deserved," Ruth spat. Pure rage drove her. "Sleeping with a man before marriage, and Louisa, I knew what she was doing. She lied to my face many times but I could see she was no longer clean."

She had invited Louisa for dinner that night, had fed her the Rohypnol she'd gotten from a man on a street corner, and had fed the mixture to Louisa as she had Aimee. Her plan being that Louisa would go to sleep and never wake up. Only she hadn't given Louisa enough, and had followed her to the club where she had waited, having grabbed a knife from her kitchen. Ruth hadn't made the same mistake with Aimee, ensuring quick results by tripling the dosage. She would finally finish the task she'd started almost thirty years earlier. She will end Aimee's pitiful life.

***

Her mother raised the frying pan again and the look in her eyes left no doubt in Aimee's mind that she intended it to be the last. Aimee pushed off from the ground, fighting dizziness and charged into Ruth, knocking the frying pan from her hand.

The stairs looked like such a long way down, and Aimee was so tired. Why couldn't she just go to sleep and worry about descending later?

Must get out. Must get help.

The words inside her head shocked her into movement. She had completely forgotten for a second why she was there and what was happening, why it was imperative to get her arse out of that fucking house. Ruth had gone crazy. She slumped against the railing, leaning heavily as she slowly made her way down, one agonising step at a time. The voice inside her head offered her encouragement the entire way.

She heard Ruth behind her, and Aimee knew it would only be a matter of time before she caught up. In her weakened state, she wouldn't be able to protect herself. Her only chance of survival was getting out onto the street. Aimee didn't dare look back, her entire concentration on moving, something about left, right, and left again. Her knees were determined to give out, her body feeling like lead as her nails dug into the wood of the banister.

"See what you're making me do, Aimee? I

wouldn't have to do this if you weren't a whore."

Aimee moved awkwardly as if unable to perform the simple task, her body failing her at her most desperate hour.

Hysteria bubbled like fine champagne in her belly. She pushed herself to move faster. Ruth was spry for her age, having already covered half the ground Aimee had spent the better part achieving.

She trembled, finding it more difficult to remain upright as it hit home that she really was forgetting the simple and automatic movements.

Her knee gave way and she fought to hold onto the railing, her hand, heavy, fell to her side. With nothing to hold onto, Aimee pitched forward, her feet coming out from under her as she missed the next step and tumbled down the stairs. A hard step jarred her jaw as another hit her elbow, her actions not quick enough to protect her head and pain exploded on impact before she rolled onto the flat surface below. The blissful darkness overcame and she obediently succumbed as the extent of her injuries hit her.

Chapter 44

Ruth stared down at her unconscious daughter. Such a shame. She had expected a peaceful and happy life, and instead she got a man who fucked her and defiled her body, and two tramps for daughters—their father's daughters. She'd shown them, hadn't she? Every single one of them, starting with her beloved husband twenty-five years earlier.

After she'd fed him rat poison, he'd suffered immensely, choking as he gasped for air. With pleasure, she'd told Steven what he had ingested as soon as the symptoms started to show, and it was too late for him. She had despised his lovemaking, and knew as a married woman the only way she would ever be free of such a degrading duty was to be rid of her husband. Under the cover of darkness, she had buried him in the backyard, six feet down, and planted the most gorgeous rose bush over top. When she saw the white beauty of those flowers, she remembered the ugliness that had brought them about.

No one had questioned her when she'd

announced that he'd left them in the middle of night. It had been so easy. Easier than she'd anticipated.

She was doing everyone a favour, including Aimee, who'd strayed so far off the righteous path. She didn't fear the repercussions. God would still welcome her into his Kingdom, and she had prayed to him countless times over the years, describing how she felt, what she needed to do.

And everybody knows God helps those who help themselves.

Ruth descended the stairs slowly, her illness beginning to take a toll on her. The doctors had done their best, but she was far too advanced for them to completely cure her. Soon, it would all be over, and she would be free and at peace. Ruth gripped the handle of the stainless steel knife she'd retrieved from her undergarment drawer. The sharp blade was effective, and she'd used it on Louisa with no trouble, despite her age and condition.

She was halfway down the stairs when her front door burst open, splinters of wood flying in all directions, and if she'd had the strength Ruth would've scolded the six officers who invaded her house, their weapons drawn. But she was tired and all she wanted to do was finish the job she'd started. She hadn't heard them pull up, nor had she heard the sirens, and wasn't surprised when she glanced out her window to see several police vehicles parked on her lawn, none with their sirens on or their lights flashing. She frowned at the cars. Her beautiful lawn. How could they just park on it? Couldn't they see the time and effort she had put into it? Did they not care?

What would her neighbours think? She had tried to be a good, courteous, friendly neighbour over the years. God knew it hadn't been easy, what with the tenuous neighbours she had been given. Her standing as a single mother hadn't helped, but the fact she was friendly to the women and ignored the men had made it easier. When people needed sugar or milk, she was the one they came to. But no one ever bothered her for anything else. A few times, she had to ask people to turn their music down or move their bins and pick up after their pets, but otherwise she was well-liked.

Even now, Ruth caught the curious glances from her neighbours as they exited their houses, mothers with children on their hips, phones in their hands.

Enjoy the show. This was the first time she'd been in control of her own life. She'd been Steven's wife, then a mother. Never Ruth. Her gaze fell to her daughter, lying there unconscious, appearing almost innocent, but Ruth knew better.

"Ruth, put the weapon down," Detective Hill ordered.

She frowned at the man, not wanting to disobey him, but couldn't do as he asked. He'd arrived earlier than she had expected. He was supposed to show up *after* they found Aimee's body, not before. They had obviously figured out it was her, not Aimee, who had murdered Louisa. But she didn't care. No one could touch her. No one could judge her. There was only one man who could pass judgement on her, and she knew without a doubt she would soon be joining Him.

Chapter 45

James's gaze found Aimee laying unmoving at the base of the stairs and his stomach roiled. How could he have abandoned her? He should've checked on her after she was released, made sure she was all right. He should have told her he knew her to be innocent and not to worry. He'd told her once before but maybe she thought her being arrested might've somehow changed his opinion. He holstered his Glock and ran to her, his heart pounding, his throat closed.

Let her be all right, please. Kneeling beside her, he felt for her pulse.

"Aimee?" he asked, his throat dry and his back slick with fear. He ran his hands over her body, determining for any major injuries, and cursed. She looked like she'd been to hell and back and he didn't doubt for a second that was the case. Would Aimee ever be able to get over the fact that her mother had tried to kill her, and *had* killed her sister?

Aimee was strong and didn't allow anything to

touch her, or at least she tried. She wasn't as thick-skinned and in control as she liked to believe. She was fragile, in need of cosseting.

And he loved her. He was going to make sure she knew that every day for the rest of her life.

The pulse beneath his fingertips throbbed weakly. He willed her to open her eyes, to look at him, but she didn't.

"Come on, baby," he whispered, his voice so low that only Aimee—had she been conscious—would've heard him. "Please wake up. Come on, show me those big grey eyes that send shivers down my spine. Let me know you're okay. Come on, Aimee."

***

Darryl felt calm despite the situation. Ruth's eyes narrowed at James as she made a threatening step forward, as if she didn't care that five weapons were aimed at her.

"Stay away from her," she snarled. "I know what you want from her. What you all want from us. I have to save her from herself."

"Ruth, it's over, put your weapon down," Darryl ordered.

"No!" she yelled, and her gaze fell back to Aimee as James held her close. "One more. Just one more."

This wouldn't end well and not without a ton of paperwork. He just wanted to get home, to wrap his arms around his wife and forget this case ever happened. Unfortunately for Aimee, she would never have that luxury. Damn, he hated to think of what she'd been through. She had lost her sister, she'd been treated as a suspect when she'd been nothing but helpful, and she had more than likely fallen in love with a man who might very well break her heart.

So long as they all survived.

The Ruth Burnes he'd met seemed to have vanished, and the woman in her place had a feral look on her face that said she wasn't about to go down easily. But she'd made the fatal error of bringing a knife to gun fight. A knife that Darryl guessed had been used on Louisa Burnes. The weapon still had dried blood on the edge, smudged down the side.

Ruth made another threatening move towards her daughter. She wasn't finished. Whatever Aimee had done to piss her mother off was something horrific in Ruth's estimation, and she wasn't about to back down. He hated when cases ended this way.

"Don't do it, Ruth, it's not worth your life," he warned.

She laughed, and out of the corner of his eye Darryl saw several members of his team shiver at the callous and frightening sound. Within seconds, Ruth was lunging at James and Aimee, knife poised, murder in her eyes.

Five firearms discharged. Not one of them hesitated. They saw a threat and acted accordingly, each bullet hitting its target. Ruth Burnes's body jerked back and blood seeped through her cotton shirt, the wounds severe.

Never threaten a police officer.

Ruth Burnes obviously didn't understand the notion of protecting one's own.

Her body hit the stairs as it pitched forward and rolled down the last few steps, crumpling at the bottom. James stepped clear with Aimee cradled in his arms.

Nick moved closer to the dead woman and kicked away the knife before squatting down beside her and taking her pulse, all the while accessing the situation, looking for more danger or surprises. He stood and faced the other detectives as he holstered his weapon, the others followed suit.

"Dead," he said.

Darryl nodded, watching as James cradled Aimee in his arms, holding her close to his chest. His lips moved but Darryl couldn't make out the words he was saying.

He spoke into his phone, organising the forensic team to sweep the scene, an ambulance for Aimee, and for Doctor Stone to come and remove Ruth's body. Then he turned his back on the scene and found himself staring out the window. A crowd had gathered. Sirens blared in the distance. Had one of the neighbours called for police when they'd heard gunshots? Listening to the dispatcher speak, he figured that was so, and one of the sirens belonged to an ambulance that would arrive in under two minutes.

Darryl craned his neck toward James. When he had the detective's attention, he held up two fingers, indicating how long it would take for the ambulance to arrive. By the look on James's face, it couldn't be soon enough. Aimee needed immediate medical attention.

When Stone told him he'd be there shortly, and the head of the forensics team assured him they were on the way, Darryl hung up and dialled another number. He needed to tell his wife he wouldn't be home for dinner.

Chapter 46

James kissed Aimee's forehead near the small, angry cut where a dried crimson stain remained around the mark. Occasionally, she whimpered, her body fighting whatever had been done to it. It was certainly a shock to her system and he guessed a dose of Rohypnol—hell, why change something that worked, right? If Ruth had subdued Louisa with the drug, why not Aimee? Only, his Aimee was one hell of a fighter. One who didn't back down.

His Aimee. That had a nice ring to it. He only hoped she was conducive to the idea because he wasn't going anywhere. He planned to tell her as soon as she was likely to remember the conversation.

"It's all over, Aimee," he said, hugging her as tight as he dared without worrying that he was hurting her.

He had no idea how substantial her injuries were and until he did he had to be extremely careful in case he aggravated something he shouldn't. In fact he shouldn't even be holding her now. She should be laying down but the fear that Ruth would hurt her had put all his protective instincts into high alert and he'd removed her out of harm's way. Now she was in his arms for his sake not hers. He needed to feel her close to him. Feel her heart beat and the warmth of her body telling him she was alive. He let out a deep breath, one he'd been holding since he'd arrived and saw Aimee, defenceless and all alone at the bottom of the stairs with a deranged woman wielding a knife above her.

"It's all over," he said, although he wasn't sure if he'd said that to comfort her or himself.

***

Aimee moved her head slightly. The pain from the frying pan threatened to implode her head. She was sure she was going to be sick and her whole body throbbed painfully, probably from her flight down the stairs. She couldn't open her eyes, couldn't even try. She drifted in and out of consciousness and while she wasn't entirely sure what happened. All she knew was James had his arms around her. His scent filled her nostrils and left her feeling safe.

He had come for her. The thought that rocketed through her pounding head made her warm with fuzzy feelings. If she wasn't so tired Aimee knew she would've cried and probably would when she regained her equilibrium and relived the emotion of having James come to her rescue—at him holding her close as if he never intended to let go.

"Thank you," she whispered, unsure if he heard

her. Her voice was faint, so faraway it seemed like it was a stadium away from her. The small sound causing pain to explode in her ear beside the largish bump beginning to grow beneath her hair.

The only reply she got was the tightening of his arms around her.

Epilogue

Relaxed, Darryl enjoyed the small party the group had thrown together, hugging his wife against him.

"I would like to make a toast. To one of Harbour Bay's finest superintendents ever," Matt said, as his daughter reached out from her perch on her mother's hip, demanding to be picked up. Matt chuckled and switched the flute to his other hand as he lifted the nine-month-old into his arms. The little imp snuggled into her father and smiled.

Or at least Darryl assumed it was a smile. Knowing Miss Madeline Murphy, it could've been anything—usually ending with a change of a nappy. His gaze wandered around the room as they all raised their glasses and took a sip of the champagne. Hallie stood beside Natalie and Kellie. Amelia was leaning against the refreshment table with James, and Nick and Dean were both next to him. Caitlyn Harris glowed with happiness beside her husband, her arm around his waist.

They were all standing in the conference room

on the second floor. Someone—most likely Caitlyn with the help of Natalie and Kellie—had decorated the room with balloons and streamers and more importantly food and alcohol. It had been three months since the day Aimee had been attacked by her mother, and she seemed to be recovering well from her near-death experience.

James had remained by her side, even going as far as fighting with the hospital staff when he refused to step outside as the doctors examined her, despite her forehead cut only requiring a butterfly bandage and a couple of aspirins. She'd then been signed in as a patient for monitoring until the Rohypnol was out of her system and her mild concussion subsided.

With the closure of the case, and James having proved himself as one of the team, he'd been welcomed as such. No one held Aimee against him, and even Darryl was relieved at knowing his gut reaction had been right. Aimee had been innocent, and she hadn't been trying to manipulate them for her own agenda—except maybe James. She certainly had designs on him.

The murder of Carolyn Harper remained unsolved but never forgotten. The team didn't believe in allowing a case to cool, and they worked new angles every day and sought out leads in hopes of finding her killer. One thing was for certain, none of them believed he was finished, and they felt another victim would be found soon enough.

"I would also like to take this opportunity to officially announce Amelia Donovan as my replacement," Alec Harris stated. Again, glasses went up and they each took another sip.

Kellie squealed with delight and rushed to her best friend, wrapping her arms around her. Knowing his wife as he did, she was probably squeezing her tightly, perhaps *too* tightly. He noticed a mixture of relief and excitement in Amelia's eyes as she returned the embrace.

Aimee was standing outside the door, appearing nervous, the business wear she had favoured gone and in its place was a bright floral maxi-dress that clung to her breasts before widening from her waist down, flaring about her ankles. The floral pattern on her dress featured a smorgasbord of daisies, dandelions, and lilies. Her long hair was loose about her shoulders, falling down her back and over her breasts, a pair of Dior sunglasses keeping the chestnut tresses from her face.

Darryl moved toward her, a genuine smile on his face. He hadn't seen her since her time in the hospital. He and Kellie had visited her a couple times. The first time had been to get her statement, and the second visit had been because he wanted to make sure she would be okay. Both times, he'd practically tripped over James.

Over the past couple of months, Darryl had been delighted to discover every thought he'd had about her character had been backed by action. Aimee Burnes was a great woman. Kind and sweet, beautiful inside and out.

"Aimee."

She shifted nervously. "Detective Hill, hello. James asked me to meet him here. That's all right, isn't it?"

"Of course. You're always welcome here. How are you?"

The wariness in her eyes dissipated and she relaxed. It surprised him to see the once confident woman self-conscious. James had mentioned her hang-ups. Did she think they believed her presence somehow sullied them?

"I'm fine, thank you."

"You're holding up okay?"

"Yes. It's still all so strange, like it never happened, you know? Sometimes I wake up and think it's all a dream, but then I remember."

He nodded solemnly. The truth of her father's abandonment had been revealed during the investigation into her mother when a diary of Ruth's had been discovered, detailing her involvement and Steven Burnes's body had been recovered from the backyard beneath a rose bush, no doubt near where Aimee and her sister had played as children.

"So, do you have any plans on where you go from here?"

"Well, I'm actually thinking about selling the club."

"Really?" he asked, surprised.

Her hand tightened on the purse strap that hung from her shoulder. "Yeah, it just isn't what it used to be to me."

Darryl gave her a sad smile. "I can imagine that. Do you know what you're going to do without it?"

Aimee half shrugged. "No specifics at the moment, but I ran a successful business, so I doubt I'll lack for opportunities. But I'm going to take some time, make sure my next decision is the right one."

"Good luck to you. Hawke tells me you're moving in together."

She smiled radiantly which told him more than words. "We're going to give it a try. See where it leads."

"Good. You both deserve happiness."

She flushed. "I hear you're expecting a baby?"

He unconsciously puffed out his chest. "Kellie is due in seven months."

"Congratulations. You must be excited."

"Thank you. I am…and a little terrified. But I'm not alone. Kellie and I will work it out."

"I'm sure you will."

He caught James's gaze over his shoulder as the younger man spoke with Nick and Dean and indicated towards Aimee with a nod of the head. James smiled. He wasn't smiling at Darryl. It was a smile reserved for only one person, a private smile shared with a lover. He said goodbye to the men who followed him out into the hall.

"Hey."

"Hey yourself, Detective," Aimee replied, her gaze softening.

James leaned down and kissed her lightly on the lips. A hello kiss, nothing more. Only the hand placed possessively on Aimee's waist and the heated look in the man's eyes gave any indication as to how he felt.

Aimee snuggled against his side. Darryl doubted Aimee realised how much she leaned against James and the level of trust she'd placed in him. She most definitely wasn't the same woman he'd met at the club all those months ago. The Aimee then would've probably denied ever needing anyone and he'd noticed she was quick to smile around James— and that smile was blinding in its beauty.

"Aw, shit. Another one bites the dust." Dean's comment had James and Aimee frowning. "I swear, Matt cursed us."

Darryl laughed.

"Wanna run that by me?" James asked.

Years ago at Matt and Natalie's wedding, the groom had turned to them and told them they were next. After he'd fallen in love with Kellie, Dean had started to get that hunted look in his eyes and obviously believed Matt to be the catalyst.

Personally, Darryl couldn't wait until Dean met his match. It was going to be amusing seeing him hung up over a woman.

"Don't worry about it," Nick said, and held out his hand to Aimee. "Nick Doyle."

Aimee shifted against James to shake Nick's hand.

"Sorry. I'd forgotten you haven't been formally introduced. Aimee Burnes, Detectives Nick Doyle and Dean Matthews. They were there that day."

They all heard the words Hawke didn't say. *The day your mother tried to kill you and instead ending up being shot by the cops—the very men surrounding you.*

Aimee nodded politely to Nick and Dean who both stared at her in obvious interest.

James turned to him. "We're going to head off. Tell Harris I'll see him around and congratulate Donovan for me. I'll see you all tomorrow."

He nodded. "Enjoy yourselves."

Aimee's gaze locked onto him, a wealth of emotion swirling in the grey depths. "Thanks—for everything," she said. Then she turned towards Dean and Nick. "All of you, thank you. I wouldn't be here today without you."

"You're welcome," Nick said, and Dean nodded his agreement.

James moved his hand from her waist to the small of her back and led her back to the elevator. He pressed the down button and the door opened. They stepped into the carriage and before the door closed, he leaned in and kissed her head.

Darryl smiled. James was clearly smitten and Aimee had a glow about her which would make many jealous.

He returned to the conference room and found his wife. Kellie was barely showing except for a small bulge hidden beneath her clothes. After the day they'd rescued Aimee, Darryl had wondered what was holding him back. He thought about how nothing was certain in this life and that the most important thing was the family he'd envisioned with Kellie. He may be a little terrified about what was to come, but he'd have her beside him always to help him figure it out.

He was a lucky man and never planned to forget it. He glanced back over his shoulder at Nick and Dean.

Which of them would be the next to fall?

Acknowledgements

Thank you for reading, The Dead Don't Lie and to the team at Limitless Publishing who made this book possible, I'd be nowhere without your endless support. I appreciate all your hard work and look forward to future collaborations. I'd also like to thank friends, Leonie and Michael who are always helping me. I still have much to learn, but I'm slowly getting there. You indeed are the adults that are better at 'adulting' than I. I'm sure you secretly roll your eyes at my ineptness but five years and you're still around so I must be doing something right! (Probably providing you mass amounts of entertainment). I couldn't ask for better friends.

About the Author

Camille Taylor is an Australian author who resides in the Nation's Capital with her small dog. She was the typical 90's kid and was raised on Goosebumps, Roald Dahl and Paul Jennings. In her teens she began reading the Queen of Crime, Agatha Christie and in later years found Christine Feehan, Janet Evanovich and Julie Garwood.

She started writing at sixteen and enjoys spending time with her family, doting on her nieces and nephews, writing the many stories floating about her head and working on her genealogy where she can trace her heritage to England, Scotland, Ireland and Russia.

Her other interests include, anything creative—such as scrapbooking and drawing and has travelled across Western Europe, New Zealand and the UAE, after spending a year living in London. She's also dabbled in tae kwon do.

Facebook:
https://www.facebook.com/CamilleTaylorAuthor

Twitter:
https://twitter.com/CamilleTaylorAu

Website:
https://camilletaylorbooks.wordpress.com/

Goodreads:
https://www.goodreads.com/author/show/7791241.Camille_Taylor